IVY'S DELTA (SPECIAL FORCES: OPERATION ALPHA)

DELTA TEAM 3, BOOK FOUR

ELLE JAMES

Dear Readers,

Welcome to the Special Forces: Operation Alpha Fan-Fiction world!

If you are new to this amazing world, in a nutshell the author wrote a story using one or more of my characters in it. Sometimes that character has a major role in the story, and other times they are only mentioned briefly. This is perfectly legal and allowable because they are going through Aces Press to publish the story.

This book is entirely the work of the author who wrote it. While I might have assisted with brainstorming and other ideas about which of my characters to use, I didn't have any part in the process or writing or editing the story.

I'm proud and excited that so many authors loved my characters enough that they wanted to write them into their own story. Thank you for supporting them, and me!

This series is special to me as the five authors writing in the Delta Team Three series took a team that I introduced in *Shielding Kinley* and made them their own.

READ ON!
 Xoxo
 Susan Stoker

To my friend, Susan Stoker, for inviting me into her world for a fun adventure we hope you all will enjoy.
To my friends, Becca, Lynne, Riley and Lori for all the love and support throughout this joint effort. You guys rock!
To my readers who follow me everywhere. You are the reason I write. Thank you for reading my stories.
Be sure to pick up all the books in the Delta Team Three series!

Nori's Delta by Lori Ryan
Destiny's Delta by Becca Jameson
Gwen's Delta by Lynne St. James
Ivy's Delta by Elle James
Hope's Delta by Riley Edwards

CHAPTER 1

MAGNUS "DUFF" McCormick sat in the back of the CH-47 Chinook, dressed for the battle simulation, his M4A1 loaded with blanks and his vest packed with magazines full of even more blanks.

That day's training scenario was VIP extraction in rugged terrain using ultralight vehicles dropped from a Chinook helicopter. The vehicles could be dropped into any environment and had the maneuverability needed to get in and out of places that may not have roads, or that had roads that were heavily guarded and to be avoided.

Woof tapped his booted toes on the metal floor of the aircraft, his rifle balanced across his knees. "Let's get this show on the road. I'm sweatin' balls here."

Military operations in the deserts of Afghanistan could be hot. The kind of hot you feel pouring out of a pizza oven, only worse—you can't close the oven. The heat is oppressive and constant during the day.

Thankfully, they weren't currently in Afghanistan. They were on the Fort Hood Military Range. Real bullets wouldn't be flying at them, but the heat was similar to that in Afghanistan, especially in the belly of the helicopter with no doors or windows open. Today they were practicing an extraction of a very important person. In this case, it was the commanding officer of their unit. The CO.

Some of the guys thought that meant they had to be even better than good at getting him out of the fake "dangerous" situation.

Duff wasn't one of them. He did his job. It didn't matter if the target for extraction was his CO, a politician or a trained monkey. His job was to extract the target and bring him back alive in the most expedient manner possible.

"WE HIT the LZ in five mikes," Luke "Merlin" Forest called out over the roar of the chopper blades. The old man of the team, he adjusted his helmet strap and climbed into the Ultralight Tactical Vehicle, or UTV.

The rest of the men moved into position in their assigned vehicles, ready to deploy as soon as the helicopter landed.

Duff straddled the all-wheel drive 450 rugged terrain motorcycle that looked like a dirt bike but contained a bullet-resistant radiator and a much sturdier frame to withstand just about any task the Army decided to throw at it.

The Chinook slowed its forward motion and slowly dropped into position at the same time as the rear ramp lowered.

A rush of hot air and wind replaced the stagnant heat. His adrenaline pumping, Duff started the engine and revved the throttle.

"Duff," Merlin shouted. "Wait for the fucking chopper to land. Do you hear me?" He raised his voice, yelling over the roar of the helicopter's dual blades whipping the air. "You know the CO doesn't like personnel dying on training missions. Too damned much paperwork."

Duff nodded. "I've got this." He had thousands of hours of experience riding dirt bikes. It was what he did when he had any time off. The more rugged the terrain and the faster he could go, the better. He'd broken every rib in his body at one time or another. They'd healed and they would again.

Adjusting his helmet one last time, he narrowed his eyes and studied the terrain as the helicopter descended.

When the ramp was still five feet off the ground, Duff twisted the throttle, opening it wide, let his foot off the brake and rocketed out of the helicopter's bowels.

As he left the back of the chopper, he pulled up on the handlebars and came down hard on his back tire.

The motorcycle fishtailed. He skimmed a booted foot across the ground, steadied and took off in the direction of the target on terrain he'd studied prior to climbing aboard their transport.

A quick glance over his shoulder showed the ramp touching ground and the two ultralight tactical vehicles blasting out of the back, loaded with his teammates, racing to catch up to him.

Duff returned his focus to the task ahead.

Roads existed that would take him to his quarry, but they weren't the most direct route, and they were lined with improvised explosive devices and guards, according to the scenario. Instead, he chose to go cross-country, dropping down into a ravine and popping back up on the other side, both wheels flying four feet above the ground before gravity brought him back to earth.

"Remember you have a team back here," Merlin ground out, his voice crackling in Duff's headset.

"Gotcha," Duff said.

"Fucking asshole. Gonna get yourself killed," Merlin muttered.

"Yeah, and who would care?" Duff retorted.

"No one," Woof said. "But one or all of us would have to risk our necks to bring you home. You know that old saying, no man left behind?"

Duff slowed slightly. He'd been in a battle where

he'd had to carry a team member out. A lifeless member. One he was supposed to cover while he'd leaped forward during an operation in urban terrain. His teammate had leaped into an ambush.

No matter how many bullets he'd pumped into the air above that building, Duff hadn't been able to stop the Taliban rebel from killing his friend. He'd had to carry the man's body out and face his wife and kids when they'd returned Stateside.

Slowing a little more, he waited for the others to come in range before he took off again.

Once his teammates engaged, he would circle around the aggressors, get in and extract their target. Hopefully, his CO would be agreeable to riding out on the back of the dirt bike. It wasn't the best way to leave, but it got them out when the aggressors outnumbered them four to one. And they couldn't shoot them. It was, after all, an exercise, not the real deal.

Depending on the physical status of the person to be extracted, the bike was more maneuverable, could get in and out with a smaller footprint and was not as easily picked out of the shadows as a UTV.

As he neared the Combined Arms Collective Training Facility, he swung wide, keeping to the tree line until he was close to the back entrance of the mockup of a Middle Eastern village.

Their intel had located their target in the

embassy. All he had to do was sneak in with his team, take out a few bad guys and extract their VIP.

Though the rooftops of the mockup buildings were concrete and could support a helicopter landing, they had chosen to train under the assumption the rooftops weren't strong enough. They would have to drop in close to the village, move in on ATVs or motorcycles and go the rest of the way on foot.

At the predesignated location, Duff paused in the shadows of the scrubby trees at the edge of the training site. So far, the aggressor forces had not engaged him.

"In position," he reported.

"Hold until we give you the signal," Merlin responded.

"Roger." Duff's adrenaline spiked through his system, making it difficult for him to wait. He needed action.

"Going in to stir the pot," Merlin said. He would lead the first UTV into the city, drop some of his men from the vehicle and race past the embassy to distract the aggressors while the men on foot stormed the flanks and rear of the compound, taking out as many of the guards as possible.

Duff waited, straining his ears for the sound of gunfire.

When it came, he revved the engine and waited for his cue.

"Duff, you're on," Merlin said.

Duff released the brake and raced into the village and up to the back of the embassy where his teammates had secured the entrance.

Rather than dismount and enter on foot, Duff ran the motorcycle up the steps and through the door into the shell of a building, spun the bike around and nodded to his teammates who were protecting their CO as he ran toward Duff.

"Hop on!" Duff called out.

"You're kidding me, right?" his CO said, his brow rising.

"No, sir," Duff said. "Fastest way out. Come with me if you want to live," he said.

The CO climbed onto the back of the bike.

"Hold on," Duff yelled. Before the CO had his arms all the way around his waist, Duff took off, shooting out the back door and down the steps.

His commander clamped his arms around Duff's waist and held on as they flew through the streets. Duff's teammates were staged at every corner to provide cover for the departing duo.

Moments later, Duff blasted out of the village and headed for the tree line, zigzagging to give any aggressor on a rooftop less of a chance of firing a kill shot at them.

Entering the shadows of the trees, Duff didn't slow, but dodged the low-hanging branches of the mesquites, heading for the extraction point where the helicopter was scheduled to pick up its cargo.

When Duff burst out into the open, the Chinook was there, ramp down and ready.

Duff sped up.

"Slow the fuck down," his CO yelled in his ear.

Duff heard but chose to ignore him. He raced across the field, slowing at the last possible moment, bumped up the ramp, stopped and jerked his head toward one of the gunners. "Get him off."

As soon as the CO was off the back of the bike, Duff sped out of the chopper and back toward the village.

The two UTVs emerged from the trees, members of his team clinging to the roll bars.

Duff slowed, tipped the bike over on its side, and laid down protective fire for his team as they ran their vehicles up the ramp into the Chinook.

When the last UTV was in, Duff lifted his bike, gunned the throttle and turned it as he slung his leg over the seat.

The propeller blades at each end of the Chinook beat the air in preparation for takeoff.

Duff twisted the throttle, giving the bike all it could take and entered the back of the chopper, skidding to a sideways halt. The ramp started up and the Chinook lifted off the ground.

"What if I'd been incapacitated?" The CO came at him, as Duff climbed off the back of the dirt bike.

"We were prepared to take you out in one of the UTVs," Duff answered. "We knew our target was agile and capable of holding onto the back of the motorcycle."

"And if the enemy had roughed me up so that I couldn't?"

Duff lifted his chin. "Again, we would have taken you out on one of the UTVs."

The CO rubbed his backside. "You could have waited until I was down the back steps before loading me onto the bike." His lips twitched. "That was a helluva ride."

Duff nodded. "Yes, sir."

His commander's eyes narrowed. "You're lucky it was me."

"Yes, sir."

The CO turned to the team in the back of the Chinook. "Good job. Next time might be for real. I want an after-action report of the exercise, including your review of the use of Ultralight Tactical Vehicles, in the extraction scenario. Right now, I want your thoughts. Give me the pros."

"They're better equipped to handle rough terrain," Jangles said.

Zip grinned and patted the side of the UTV he'd ridden on. "They're lightweight and agile."

Woof snorted. "Got us in there faster than going in on foot."

The commander crossed his arms over his chest. "Cons?"

"They aren't hardened for IEDs." Merlin shook

his head. "But then, they're lighter. You can't have it both ways."

The CO turned to Duff. "And the bike?"

"Fast." Duff shrugged. He was ready to get back to the unit and out of uniform. The heat was making him crankier than usual. "Need both hands on the handlebars so it puts the rider at a disadvantage with weapons."

"But it can fly," Jangles said. "At least with Duff it can."

The commander's brow twisted. "You mean it's fast?"

"Yes, sir, but it really can fly." Zip's grin broadened. "Right, Duff?"

Duff glared at the members of his team. "I knew what I was doing. We got the VIP out, didn't we?"

"Yes, you did," the CO said. "The dirt bike and the UTVs are still intact. They'll live to serve another day."

The Chinook slowed and hovered before lowering to the ground.

"Good job, men." Their commander said. "You're dismissed...after you complete your after-action reports."

The men groaned.

Merlin gave the CO a chin lift. "We'll see you at the Ugly Mug?"

Their commander shook his head. "Sorry. The wife has other plans for me."

"Let us guess." Jangles tipped his blond head. "Lawn mowing or watching the kids while the wife goes out with her gal pals?"

The CO's lips twisted. "Both."

Duff shook his head, glad he didn't have a woman calling the shots for him. One less person to answer to was always a good thing.

The commander was first out of the chopper after it landed.

"Ugly Mug, 7:00 pm," Merlin announced. "That includes, you, Duff."

Duff frowned. "I was thinking of taking my dirt bike out to the track for some exercise."

"It's Donovan's farewell party," Merlin said. "He and his team are coming. They expect us to be there to give the guy a proper send-off."

"Why he's giving up a perfectly good career, pounding dirt and eating bullets, is beyond me," Duff muttered.

Merlin gave Duff his killer glare. "He and his team have saved our butts on numerous occasions. You can do this for him."

"And we've returned the favor," Duff pointed out.

"Look, you're not backing out on me now," Merlin said through tight lips. "Gwen's bringing a friend for you."

Duff's frown deepened. "All the more reason to skip the Ugly Mug tonight."

"You promised you'd be there. You always said

your word is golden." Merlin's lips thinned. "And how's Gwen's friend going to feel if you're a no-show?"

Duff shrugged. "I don't know her. Why should I care?"

Merlin drew in a deep, measured breath and let it out slowly. "You won't disappoint her, because beneath that gruff exterior is a heart the size of Texas."

Jangles, Zip and Woof all burst out laughing.

"I want some of whatever whacky weed you've been smokin'," Zip said. "Gruff Duff is about the least sympathetic man you'll ever meet."

"Got that right," Duff agreed.

"Hey, Duff." Jangles' brow twisted. "Have you even had a date in the past ten years?"

Duff slung his rifle over his shoulder, mounted the motorcycle, and let his lip curl in a hint of a sneer. "If I had, I sure as hell wouldn't tell you guys."

"Fine, dude. I didn't want to play my ace card," Merlin said, "but, dammit Duff, you owe me."

Duff frowned. "What the hell are you talking about?"

"That time in Fallujah when I saved your ass from the rooftop sniper." Merlin crossed his arms over his chest. "That ought to count for something."

His frown deepening, Duff narrowed his eyes. "We've all saved each other's asses so many times, we're square." He pushed the bike down the ramp.

"But, for Gwen, I'll be there." He shot a glare over his shoulder. "For the record, I don't like being set up."

"Someone had to do it," Zip followed him out of the chopper. "Or you'll die a lonely, grumpy old man."

"Ever consider I might like being alone?" Duff grumbled.

"Yeah, but we're all hoping a woman can smooth your rough edges and make you a little less of an asshole," Woof said. "I'm bringing Nori. She's looking forward to seeing Duff take the fall for a female."

Duff swung a fist at him with little intention of hitting the man.

Woof ducked with a grin. "See you at seven." He turned to Zip. "You're bringing Destiny?"

Zip nodded. "Wild horses couldn't keep her from witnessing the big man's fall."

"I'm not going to fall," Duff muttered. "I don't even know the woman."

Merlin chuckled. "Famous last words."

Duff stowed the bike in the motor pool and headed out. He wanted to get in a good hour on weights and a four-mile run. If he felt like it, he might show up at the Ugly Mug. Not that he was looking forward to meeting his "date".

CHAPTER 2

"I SHOULDN'T HAVE COME," Ivy Fremont said, smoothing her hand over her hair, trying to keep the Texas wind from blowing it into a tangled mess. "I've never been to a bar frequented by military guys."

"They won't bite. Unless you want them to. Besides, you needed to get out." Gwen pushed her glasses up her nose and her bright red hair behind her ears. "And us redheads have to stick together, right?"

Ivy smiled at her friend. "You really like this guy, don't you?"

Gwen sighed. "Luke is amazing."

"Like the prince charming in one of your classic fairytales you sell in your bookstore?"

Gwen shook her head. "Oh, hell no. He's hero material. The red, white and blue, got your back, put his life at risk kind of hero that makes you go weak at the knees. All of his teammates are like that. That's why I thought you needed to meet them. One in particular."

Ivy sighed. "I don't mind going to the bar as much as being set up on a blind date."

Gwen raised an eyebrow. "What happened to the happy, free spirit you swore you were going to be? I thought you'd moved on from the uptight woman you were when you were arguing criminal cases in court?"

Ivy sighed. "I'm fine when I'm at my shop surrounded by dreamcatchers, beautiful clear glass and incense. It's such a different world that I can push my past behind me and forget, for a few minutes, that I was once a high-powered attorney on my way up in my law firm."

"Do you regret giving it all up?" Gwen asked.

"Not for a moment. I didn't have the balls of steel needed to put animals behind bars for life." That hollow feeling in her gut threatened to take over and pull her to her knees.

Gwen touched her arm. "You can't blame yourself for what happened."

"How could I not blame myself?" she said. "He got off because I botched the case. The jury set him free and he killed the woman I'd sworn to protect. A woman he'd already molested once. I convinced her to testify, despite her desire to walk away."

"Her death wasn't in vain," Gwen reminded her.

"Had she not testified, they might never have known who it was. He could have killed her anyway and then gone on to kill others."

Ivy knew what Gwen said was true. "Still, if I'd done my job right, he'd have gone to jail for rape. He wouldn't have been free to hurt her again."

"You don't know that." Gwen stared across the parking lot at the door to the Ugly Mug Bar. "Tonight, you need to put it all behind you. Have a little fun. Remember who you are. The Ivy Fremont who owns a gift store. You're no longer going to be the stiff lawyer your mother always expected you to be."

"I'm working on that." She looked down at the flowing, colorful skirt that would make her mother, the US senator, cringe. "I think I've convinced the patrons of my gift store that I'm a free spirit."

Gwen's lips twisted. "Yeah, well, you haven't convinced *me*. And I don't think you've entirely convinced yourself."

"I don't know what you're talking about. Life is short. You have to live every day like it could be your last."

Gwen nodded. "Live those words, girl. All the more reason to embrace change and meet some new people."

"You mean the guy you set me up with?" Ivy drew in a deep breath. "You're right. I need to be open to possibilities."

"And he's not another lawyer or politician like your mother wanted you to marry."

"All the better," Ivy said with a frown. "Although, I'm not in this blind date thing to marry. I'm here to have fun."

Gwen shook her head. "You're going to have to work on your expressions. You don't look like you're having fun. That frown would scare off any smart man."

"Maybe I'm not after a smart man. I've had my fill of smart guys. They can pass the bar and talk a convincing line, but their hearts never seem to be in the right place."

"Well, I can tell you, the guys you're meeting tonight are nothing like what your mother would consider appropriate for her only daughter."

"I'm liking them already." Ivy forced a smile. "But I'm not going home with my date. I'm just here for the company."

"Deal," Gwen said. "Tell you what, if you don't like the guy I set you up with, you only have to have one drink, and you don't have to stay. You can leave whenever you like. You can take my car. I can ride home with Merlin. I'd planned on doing that anyway."

Ivy smiled. "You like him a lot, don't you?"

Gwen's smile lit her face. "I love him. I don't think I've ever been this happy with a man. Can I help it I want my friends to be as happy as I am?"

"Gwen, you're a hopeless romantic."

"I haven't always been. Meeting the right person made me that way."

"How did you know he was the right one for you?"

"Ivy, you'll know." Gwen pulled open the door to the Ugly Mug Bar and held it for Ivy. "Who knows? Tonight might be your lucky night. You might just meet the man of your dreams."

"I doubt it," Ivy said. "I doubt that man actually exists."

"Live your words and be open to the possibilities." Gwen gripped her arm and gave her a gentle shove over the threshold and into the bar.

Military guys. What did she have in common with military guys?

Nothing. She'd grown up as the daughter of a political figure from the day she started kindergarten in a private school to the day she walked across the stage to collect her law degree. And she would have followed that path to the day she died, if she hadn't come to her senses.

Law fascinated her, but she'd seen too much of the corruption in the legal system. And politics was a huge factor. She'd seen her father, then her mother stretch their political muscle on several occasions to squash their rivals. Fairly and unfairly.

When she'd argued the unfairness, they'd told her the ends justified the means.

Her father had passed away from a massive heart attack at the end of his gubernatorial stint as the governor of Texas.

Her mother had run for the position and secured it, leading the state with an iron hand and progressive outlook. When her time in office came to an end, she ran for senate and was elected based on her reputation as the straight-talking governor of the great state of Texas.

"What do you hear from the senator?" Gwen asked as if reading Ivy's mind.

"My mother hasn't spoken to me since I quit the firm and bought the gift shop in Copperas Cove."

Gwen shook her head. "Doesn't she understand that family is everything? You don't always have to agree. You just have to respect each other and the decisions we make."

Ivy's lips lifted in a half-smile. "Not in my mother's books. You're either for or against what she believes. If you're against, she doesn't want anything to do with you." Ivy shrugged. "I've made several attempts to connect with her. Her aides say she's in a meeting or out of the office. When I call at night, she doesn't answer her cellphone."

Gwen leaned over and hugged Ivy as they stepped into the bar. "That's awful. I'm sorry."

"Me, too. If she wants to see me, she knows where I live." Ivy squared her shoulders and smoothed her hair back. "But we're here to have fun and be cheerful. Show me this blind date you think will be perfect for me."

Gwen gave her a sideways glance. "I didn't say perfect, but it's better than sitting home alone every night. I've met him a couple times. He's the strong, silent type from what I can tell."

"Good. At least I won't have to listen to him go on about fishing, hunting, or the latest truck he drives." She frowned. "If he doesn't talk much, how will I get to know him?"

"He might open up on the dance floor."

Ivy shook her head. "How many men do you know like to dance?"

"We're in a country bar. Men who like country music generally like dancing to it." Gwen frowned. "At least I think they do."

"So, you've set me up with a man who may or may not like to dance and doesn't talk much. The night is looking more desperate with each passing minute. Hopefully, he's at least nice to look at since he doesn't have much to say."

Ivy hoped he was as attractive as the guy she'd run into at Gwen's bookstore a week ago. "He doesn't have to be cute, but well-built. Not too full of himself would be nice." Ivy had meant to ask Gwen who the guy was, but Gwen had been busy with another customer. By the time Gwen had freed up, the man had disappeared carrying a vintage book about how to rebuild small engines. Based on his calloused fingers, he worked with his hands. So refreshing and earthy.

"Oh, he's nice to look at, if you like the built-like-a-grizzly, silent type."

"Actually, I like the idea of dating a man who doesn't do all the talking. I've worked with, and dated, more than my share of guys who thought a woman should hang on their every word. Quiet is underrated."

"Then tonight's your lucky night." Gwen's mouth turned up in a smile. "Ah, there's Luke, now." She raised her hand in greeting.

Ivy squinted in the dim lighting. There were a lot of people in the bar. She couldn't tell who Gwen was waving at.

A man with graying temples, broad shoulders and a sexy military bearing stood and waved back.

"Is that Luke?" Ivy smiled. "Wow. I see why you're attracted to him. Are all his friends in that good of shape?"

"Yes, ma'am." She grinned. "Your date is the man with his back to us, getting up from the table across from him."

The man she indicated straightened, a couple inches taller with even broader shoulders than Luke.

"Oh, my," Ivy whispered. "Are all military guys this...this...muscular?"

Gwen laughed. "Not all. These guys are part of the

Army Special Forces. They're the elite forces they send in on special missions."

Her stomach flipped and butterflies set up shop inside. She'd met only one man who'd been this big, this strong and this intimidating. And that had been in Gwen's bookstore, of all places. Just a few short days before, she'd ended up in his arms. Strong, thickly corded, muscular arms. And they'd kissed. Sweet Jesus. She'd kissed a stranger in a bookstore. Her only saving grace was that she hadn't known him, and he hadn't known her. In a state as big as Texas, it wasn't likely they'd run into each other again. Was it?

"I don't know. I've never dated anyone so...big. Are you sure it's safe?"

"Honey," Gwen said. "You're as safe as you'll ever be when you're with one of the team. Come on, let's go meet him." She hooked Ivy's arm and led her toward the table full of men.

As they approached, he turned and the light from overhead shined down on the man's face.

Ivy gasped and came to a complete standstill, bringing Gwen to an abrupt halt.

Gwen frowned. "What? Please don't say you're having second thoughts so soon. We're here. He's seen you. You at least have to say hello."

Yes, she was having second thoughts. Huge second thoughts. The man in front of her was the man she'd kissed in the stacks at the back of the Camelot Rare Books & Antiquities store.

She'd fallen from a ladder while helping Gwen organize a new shipment. He'd been there to catch her. They'd kissed and parted without exchanging names.

Her cheeks heated and her hands grew clammy.

"Don't chicken out now. For all you know, this guy could be the one." Gwen tightened her grip on her arm and dragged her toward her destiny.

Ivy shook her head. Her mother's voice grumbled in her mind. *There's no such thing as destiny. You determine your path in the world by the decisions you make.*

She'd made the decision to kiss this stranger. Had that set her on a path she couldn't vary from? Hell, for all she knew, he wouldn't even remember her. She'd worn her hair up in a messy bun, dressed in jeans and a tee, and she hadn't been wearing makeup. Surely, he wouldn't remember her.

"Hey, Luke," Gwen reached the group of men first. The rest of them rose from their chairs.

Luke pulled her into his arms and kissed her soundly on the lips.

She returned the kiss and then stepped back. "Guys, this is my friend, Ivy Fremont." One by one, Gwen went around naming them, starting with her guy. "Meet my sweetie, Luke Forest."

The man with the graying temples who'd kissed

Gwen so wonderfully took Ivy's hand in a firm grip. "It's a pleasure to meet you."

"Forest is Merlin to us, because he has a magical ability to make things happen," a blond-haired man said.

Ivy smiled. "Do I call you Luke or Merlin?"

Luke shrugged. "I answer to either."

"Since you've made a smile appear magically on my friend's face, I'll call you Merlin. Nice to meet you." Ivy grinned and shook Merlin's hand.

Gwen moved to a man with dark, longish hair and hazel eyes. "Ivy, this is Heath Davis. The guys call him Woof."

Woof took her hand.

Ivy shook it. "Why do they call you Woof?"

"Because he smells like a dog," another man said.

The other men laughed.

Merlin shook his head. "He's our team dog whisperer. Everywhere we go, dogs seem to find him and become his best friend."

"I like dogs," Ivy said as she shook Woof's hand.

"Then you'll like Woof," Merlin said. "And he'll like you."

"This is Trent Hawkins, known to the team as Zip," Gwen said as she moved aside to allow a man with brown hair and brown eyes to extend his hand to Ivy.

"Nice to meet you," she said. "What's the story behind your nickname?"

"Not important," Zip answered with a grin.

"The hell it isn't," Jangles said. "He has a wicked scar that looks like a zipper on his thigh."

Ivy frowned. "I'm sorry. Does it hurt?"

Zip shook his head. "Not a bit. But it makes all the girls want to touch it."

"And the only girl who is going to touch it from now on is me," a woman said from behind Ivy.

Ivy turned to a lovely woman with light brown skin, brown hair with tight curls and rich brown-black eyes.

"This is Destiny, Zip's lady," Gwen said. "Destiny, this is Ivy."

Destiny hugged Gwen and turned to shake hands with Ivy. "Nice to meet you."

"I'll have to turn it over to Merlin to introduce these other gentlemen." Gwen waved toward several other men gathered around the large table.

"Some of these boneheads have worked with us in the past." Merlin pointed to them, one by one. "Rucker's in charge of this motley crew including Dash, Bull, Dawg, Blade, Mac and Tank. They owe us a round of beer since we kicked their asses on the obstacle course last week."

"Yeah," Rucker said. "It won't happen again."

"Keep dreaming," Merlin said. "And say hello to Ivy."

As one, the men he'd named raised a hand and said, "Hello, Ivy."

Ivy nodded. "Nice to meet you all. I'll apologize upfront. I won't remember all of your names."

"Don't worry. After a few beers, they won't remember their own names," Merlin said.

Gwen waved a hand toward a blond-haired man walking toward the group. "Ivy, meet Beau Talbot. He's another member of Merlin's team."

"That's Beau 'Jangles' Talbot," Woof said. "And, yes, the man can dance."

Jangles held out his hand. "Nice to meet you, Ivy. If things don't work out on your blind date with this guy," he nudged the man she'd kissed at the bookstore, "I'll gladly fill in."

The big man glared at him with a killer look.

A shiver of excitement rippled through Ivy as she finally turned to the man Gwen had set her up with.

"Ivy, this is Magnus McCormick," Gwen said. "The guys all call him Duff. From what I understand, it's Scottish for black."

"On account of he's always in a dark mood," Jangles said.

Zip tipped his head. "You know, I don't think I've ever seen Duff smile."

"Maybe Ivy will coax one out of him," Destiny said.

Magnus.

Ivy's cheeks heated as she held out her hand. "Nice to meet you...Magnus." She prayed he hadn't remembered her and her impetuous kiss.

"Well, then, let your blind date begin." Merlin clapped his hand on Duff's back.

Everyone stood staring at Ivy and Duff as if they were waiting for them to do something.

Ivy's cheeks burned.

The band started playing, with a sweet, slow song.

Duff touched her arm. "Wanna?" He tipped his head toward the dance floor.

Ready to escape the scrutiny of the others, she nodded. "Yes, please."

He held out his hand.

She placed hers in his and an electric current rippled up her arm and spread throughout her chest and low into her belly.

She let him lead her out onto the floor and fold her into his arms.

For the first full minute of the music, Ivy remained stiff and unbending as he led her in a two-step around the dance floor.

After the fourth lap, she finally loosened up and relaxed. "Did you find that introduction as awkward as I did?"

He nodded. "Yes, ma'am."

Her lip quirked on one side. "You don't have to call me ma'am," she said. "My name is Ivy."

"Yes, ma'am," he said and kept moving in a circle around the floor, in a surprisingly fluid motion for a man his size and breadth.

She liked the way she felt in his arms. On the

dance floor and back in Gwen's bookstore when he'd caught and held her after her fall.

So far, he hadn't mentioned their previous meeting. Ivy was safe from the embarrassment of being reminded of her actions.

The song ended and a lively line dance began.

"Drink?" he said in his gruff way.

She nodded. "A light beer would be nice."

He started to lead her back to the group at the table. Every one of the men was watching them, as well as Gwen and Destiny.

Ivy stopped on the edge of the dance floor. "If you don't mind, I'd rather go to the bar with you."

He snorted. "We're the goddamn show." He placed his hand on the small of her back and steered her toward the bar.

"Hey, Duff." A pretty bartender smiled at them.

"Hey, Hope," Duff acknowledged.

"What can I get you and your lady friend?" she asked.

Duff turned to Ivy, his eyebrow cocked.

Ivy smiled at the bartender. "Light beer."

The bartender pulled the handle of one of the beer taps, filling a clear glass mug with frothy gold liquid. She set the mug in front of Duff and glanced at Ivy. "Bottle or tap?"

"Tap is fine." Ivy turned to Duff. "You come here often?"

"Every chance they get," the bartender said. She winked at Ivy. "I'm Hope. I manage the bar."

Ivy reached across the bar and shook Hope's hand. "I'm Ivy."

Hope filled a mug and set it in front of Ivy. "You're new here. Are you Duff's girl?"

Ivy shook her head. "We just met," she said, her cheeks hot. "Blind date."

"Duff and his friends are regulars at the Ugly Mug." She smiled at Duff. "That's the first time I've seen you out on the dance floor, man. She must be special."

He grunted and raised his mug toward his friends at the table. They each raised their drinks at him, obviously still watching them. "Fucking circus sideshow."

"They mean well," Hope said and turned to help another customer.

Ivy chuckled. "I take it this blind date wasn't your idea either?"

Duff shook his head. "Merlin and Gwen, sticking their heads into other people's business."

"You didn't have to agree to the date," Ivy said, maybe a little miffed he didn't sound pleased about being set up with her but mostly because he hadn't remembered their kiss. At the same time, he might think she'd orchestrated the date, having found out who he was from Gwen. How pathetic would that make her look?

"No, I didn't have to agree," he said.

"And you don't have to stay here with me if you don't want to," she added, staring into her beer mug.

Silence stretched between them.

Ivy glanced up to find him staring at her.

"What if I want to?" he asked in his deep, resonant voice.

She raised her mug. "I'm game if you are."

He touched his mug to hers. "Game."

She shook her head. "You really don't talk much, do you?"

"Some people talk too much," he said. "I'm not one of them."

"Glad to hear that," she said and sipped her beer. "Mind if I talk a little?"

He lifted his chin. "Knock yourself out." And he drank a long swallow of his beer.

"How long have you been in the Army?" she asked.

"Twelve years," he said and drank another gulp.

She tilted her head. "I don't detect a Southern accent. Where are you from?"

"Military brat. Spent most of my childhood on various military bases, Stateside and overseas."

Ivy nodded. "That would explain the lack of a typical Texas drawl."

She drew in a deep breath and asked what she'd been dying to ask since she'd discovered her blind date was a man she'd kissed on a whim. "Did you know who they were setting you up with before you came on this date?" she asked.

His hand stopped with his mug halfway to his mouth. A slow smile started at the corners of his lips. "If you mean, did I know it was the stranger I'd kissed in Gwen's bookstore...no."

Ivy gasped, her cheeks flooding with a rush of heat. "You remembered."

He nodded. "Hard to forget."

"I'm sorry. I shouldn't have kissed... It was presumptuous of me... Oh hell. I didn't think I'd..." Her voice faded off. Ivy wished a hole would open in the floor and suck her through.

"You didn't think you'd ever see me again?" He chuckled.

Ivy took a deep drink of her beer, hoping the big mug hid the blush sure to be making her face a bright red. "No. I didn't expect to see you again."

"Neither did I," he said.

"Yet, here we are, awkward and under a microscope with our friends observing."

They turned together to see the table of men and women still staring at them.

"Can't even kiss again, to know whether or not it was a mistake the first time."

Ivy turned back toward him, heat rising up her neck and spreading through her body.

His gaze bore into hers, making goosebumps rise on her arms.

"Who said we were going to kiss again?" she asked, her normally clear, concise tone nothing more than a breathy whisper.

He lifted one shoulder. "It was the first thought on my mind when I saw you tonight."

That electric current she'd felt when he'd held her hand rippled through her again, with no contact whatsoever. Just a look from those dark, sexy eyes.

When she didn't comment, he raised his beer and drank.

Her mouth suddenly dry, Ivy drank from her mug, not tasting the icy cold beer as it ran down her throat. The alcohol numbed her nerves ever so slightly.

When the band played another slow song, Ivy met his gaze. "Wanna?" She tipped her head toward the dance floor.

A slow smile lifted the corners of his lips. He set his mug on the counter and held out his hand.

Ivy laid her hand in his and let him pull her off the barstool onto her feet.

Whatever this was igniting between them, she prayed it was two-sided. Because she sure was feeling it and wasn't ready for it to end.

CHAPTER 3

THE EVENING WAS LOOKING up for Duff with Ivy in his arms. He two-stepped around the dance floor, remembering why he enjoyed dancing so long ago.

A stab of guilt hit him in the gut. The last time he'd held a woman in his arms and danced the two-step had been with Katie, his wife. At their wedding reception.

Eight years had passed. He was a different person from the happy newlywed he'd been then. He hadn't been in the Army long, just through Ranger school and fresh from marrying his high school sweetheart.

A lot had changed since then. His marriage had lasted a total of one week. Katie had drowned in a boating accident on their honeymoon. Rather than succumb to his sorrow, Duff had pushed himself to his limits, joined Delta Force and deployed as many times as they would send him. When he wasn't deployed, he climbed mountains, sky-dived and rode his dirt bikes. Hard.

He didn't slow down. Slowing down gave him too much time to think. To second guess life choices. To miss Katie and to regret that they hadn't had the life they'd dreamed of or the half a dozen kids they'd wanted.

Holding Ivy in his arms made him slow down. He had time to think. The guilt he felt wasn't because it was Ivy and not Katie he was holding but that he liked holding Ivy. All the years since Katie's death, he'd only slept with women to satisfy his physical needs. He hadn't kissed them.

Until Ivy.

She'd been standing precariously on a step ladder, placing old books on a top shelf when he'd passed her.

The step ladder had tilted, she'd squealed and fallen.

He could do nothing other than hold out his arms and catch her.

The auburn-haired beauty had landed perfectly in his arms, hers wrapping around his neck. For a long moment, she'd stared up at him, her green eyes rounded. "Oh," she'd said, her lips forming a sexy circle.

For a long moment, she'd stared at him and he'd stared back. Then she'd tightened her arms around his neck and kissed him.

It had felt so right, he'd kissed her back.

When she opened to him, he pushed his tongue past her teeth and caressed hers in a long, sensuous glide that left him wanting so much more.

The shuffle of feet and the sound of the bell ringing over the door brought them both back to their surroundings.

"Thank you for catching me," she'd said.

He'd lowered her legs to the ground, her body sliding across his until she stood.

Her hands had rested on his chest for a brief moment. Then her cheeks reddened, and she stepped away. "Again, thank you." She leaned up, brushed her lips across his again, spun and hurried away to help a customer with her question.

He'd been so stunned by the encounter, he hadn't thought to ask for her name. When he'd finally come to his senses and looked for her, she'd disappeared.

Gwen had been so busy with a rush of customers, he hadn't wanted to bother her. Besides, she might read more into his interest than he was willing to acknowledge at the moment.

But that kiss had been the first memorable one since his last kiss with Katie. It had awakened in him feelings and desires he'd thought long dead. More than just the physical desire to have sex.

He felt as if his body and soul had come alive after a long, painful death.

And he wasn't sure he was ready for that.

"What?" Ivy looked up at him, her eyebrow rising. "Did I step on your toes?"

He frowned. "No." But he couldn't continue dancing. "It's hot in here."

She nodded. "Want to sit this one out?"

He hooked her elbow and started toward the table with his team.

"Wouldn't you rather go back to the bar?" Ivy asked, resisting the pressure on her arm.

"No." Duff had the undeniable urge to get off the dance floor, out of the bar and onto his motorcycle. He wanted to drive as fast and far away as he could get. "I'm sorry. I'm not good at this. Don't take it personally." He marched her over to the table, pulled out a chair and handed her into it.

"Was that a smile I saw on Duff's face over at the bar?" Zip asked with a grin.

Duff's jaw hardened.

"Didn't know the old guy could dance," Woof said. "I guess still waters run deep with our man Duff."

"Pull up a chair," Merlin half-stood.

"No, thank you. I have to go." Duff turned to Ivy. "Sorry." Before anyone could say anything else, he turned and left the table, the bar and hurried out to his motorcycle.

Once outside, the fresh air and the breeze helped to calm him. He sat for a long time on his bike, going over everything about meeting Ivy.

When he'd kissed her in the bookstore, he'd been

safe—or so he thought—in assuming he'd never see her again. The kiss had been a shock, but he didn't think he'd have to deal with his emotions since he was sure, in a state as big as Texas, he wouldn't run into her.

Then to see her tonight in the Ugly Mug...it changed everything. She wasn't just a passing thought, a mirage or a ghost. Ivy Fremont was real, beautiful and a threat to the wall he'd built around his heart and soul. With that first kiss, she'd forged a crack in it—a crack he couldn't reseal. He couldn't let her into his world. He wasn't good for her. Hell, he hadn't been good for Katie. She'd drowned, and he hadn't been able to do a damned thing to save her.

Then why was he sitting there? Why didn't he just fire up his engine and drive out of the parking lot and put miles of road between him and Ivy?

For the same reason he'd sprinted out of the Ugly Mug. She'd awakened in him something he could no longer ignore.

He stared at the entrance to the Ugly Mug, debating going back inside and starting over with the woman.

Hell, she'd probably tell him to fuck off. He'd dumped her.

No, she was better off without him.

Still, he couldn't bring himself to start his engine. He sat staring at the bar, willing Ivy to come out.

Then maybe he would talk to her and explain why he'd run out of the building like a scalded cat.

Knowing he was a fool, he waited. And waited.

AFTER DUFF practically ran out of the bar. Ivy sat with the team, her gaze on the exit, her head spinning with questions.

"What the hell happened to Duff?" Gwen voiced the one question foremost in Ivy's mind.

She couldn't answer. "Excuse me. I need to go to the ladies' room." Ivy pushed to her feet before she realized she had no idea where she could find the bathrooms.

Gwen stood with her and hooked her arm. "I'll show you where it is."

After they were out of earshot of the rest of Duff's Delta team, Ivy shook her head. "I don't know what happened. One minute, we were dancing and having a good time. The next, he stopped in the middle of the floor and shut down. That's the best I can explain what he did. He just shut down."

Gwen frowned. "That jerk. I'm so sorry. I had no idea he'd act that way. With most of the rest of his team all finding their significant others, Luke and I thought it would be good to set up Duff. From what Luke says, Duff's always been a loner when it comes to women. They all thought it was time he met his match, so to speak." Gwen squeezed her arm. "I'm sorry I dragged you into my first attempt at match-making. What a disaster."

"I'm fine," Ivy lied. "It's not like we knew each other. It didn't work out. At least he didn't lead me on for any longer than necessary to determine we weren't meant to be." She would have liked to know what triggered him to decide to leave her, his friends and the bar so suddenly. "Maybe he had a bad relationship at some point in his life that makes him gun shy. You know, once bitten..."

"You're being too kind." Gwen's frown deepened. "He could have at least waited to dump you until the party was over instead of humiliating you in front of his friends."

Ivy shook her head. "Really...I'm fine. It's just that the beer I drank is going right through me. But I think I will head home. I'm tired after working at the shop all day."

"I'm really sorry." Gwen fished her keys out of her purse and handed them to Ivy. "I understand if you'd prefer not to come back to the table. Just wait long enough for me to get Luke to walk you out to my car. I'd hate to add insult to injury and have someone accost you in the parking lot after I invited you to the Ugly Mug."

"I'll get the bouncer to escort me out," Ivy said. "Don't bother Luke with me. You two have fun. I'll play it safe."

"Are you sure?" Gwen's brow twisted. "I wish you

would stay. But I completely understand your desire to leave."

"I'm going home to put my feet up." Ivy forced a smile for her friend. "To me, that sounds like heaven."

"Okay, but I still would rather Luke followed you out to make sure you get to the car safely. A lone woman is always an easy target."

"If it makes you feel better, then okay." Ivy really just wanted to walk out of the building, get into Gwen's car and drive home by herself. She didn't need another person pitying her because she'd managed to scare off a big burly Delta Force soldier.

Her ego had taken a hit. Yet, she refused to feel sorry for herself. But if one more person said he or she was sorry it hadn't worked out, she might start feeling sorry for herself.

For a few short minutes, she'd thought they had something going between them.

Boy, had she been wrong. It must have been completely one-sided. She'd obviously read more into their dance and conversation about the kiss than was actually there.

"Go on, get Luke. I'll wait for him by the exit," Ivy said.

Gwen hugged her. "I really am sorry."

"Don't be," Ivy said. "You're not responsible for someone else's reaction to me."

"Yeah, but I'm responsible for bringing you here. Are you sure you don't want me to drive you home?"

"It's your car. If you don't mind picking it up at my place tomorrow, I don't mind driving myself home."

Gwen smiled. "I don't mind picking it up tomorrow. I'd like some alone time with Luke."

"Then it's settled. Have fun." Ivy entered the restroom, did her business quickly and washed up afterward. Then, with the keys to Gwen's car in hand, she headed toward the exit, making a wide berth of the table full of Delta Force soldiers.

She should have gone back to the table and joked with the others, just to prove to them she wasn't affected by Duff's sudden departure. But she couldn't. The way he left disturbed her. She wasn't sure if it was her, or if being with her had triggered something else in him.

To go from hot to cold so quickly, he had to have something else going on in that head of his.

Luke was waiting by the entrance. He smiled and opened the door for her, waiting for her to walk through.

Once outside, he walked her to the car. "Are you going to be all right driving home alone?" he asked. "I could have one of the guys follow you."

"Don't worry about me," Ivy said. "I'm used to getting around on my own." She smiled as she unlocked the car. "Go back to Gwen. You two are so good together. I'm glad you found each other."

"I'm sorry things didn't work out for you tonight."

Merlin shook his head. "I'm not sure what got into Duff. He's never flaked out like that."

"It's okay. You can't force someone to like you. We just weren't meant to be." She gave the man another smile. "Really, it's okay. I came into the evening with no expectations. I'll go home and have a nice glass of wine and forget all about it."

"Be careful. Text Gwen when you make it inside your house."

"I will," she said. "Thank you." She climbed in behind the wheel and started the engine.

Merlin waved and walked back to the bar.

Ivy put the car in gear and started to pull out of the parking space when a man sprang out of nowhere and came at her vehicle.

Ivy's first thought was that he might have broken down and needed assistance. She lifted her foot from the accelerator automatically.

The man circled his finger. "Roll down the window. I need your help."

She shook her head, unwilling to comply. She didn't know this man wearing dark clothes, with dark eyes and a ski beanie in the Texas heat. "What's wrong?" she called out through the closed window.

He leaned his hands against the car, placing something against the driver's side window. The next second, the window shattered, scattering tiny shards of glass over Ivy's hair and clothes.

"What the hell?" she cried.

Before she could smash her foot onto the accelerator, the man reached inside her door, grabbed the handle and opened it from the inside. The next thing he did was hook his hand in her seatbelt and apply the tool he'd used to break the window to cut the belt.

Fear ripped through Ivy as she slammed her foot onto the accelerator. But it was too late.

The man had her arm, pulling her from the car as it rolled forward.

He yanked her from the car seat and onto the ground.

Ivy rolled over and tried to get up, but the stranger still had hold of her arm. He pulled her toward him, bent down and flung her over his back.

With his shoulder wedged into her gut, she could barely breathe. He ran away from Gwen's car, holding firmly to her legs.

Ivy screamed and fought, trying to free her legs.

But she couldn't shake free of the man. His arms were clamped so tightly against the backs of her calves and thighs, she couldn't move them.

With her legs useless, she pounded her fists against his back and screamed as loudly as she could. "Put me down! Help! Help!"

He slowed as they neared the back of the building.

Ivy pushed against his back and twisted, trying to see where they were going. A car sat alone in the alley behind the bar, the trunk open.

She knew she had only seconds before he threw her in and took her to who knew where. No one would know she was missing until morning when Gwen came to collect her car. No one would know what had happened to her until they found Gwen's car still in the parking lot with a broken window and a cut seat belt.

Though the man was stronger and outweighed her, Ivy fought with every ounce of determination she possessed. She fought for her life.

CHAPTER 4

DUFF HAD GIVEN up watching for Ivy to leave the Ugly Mug. The whole thing was a bad idea, start to finish. Starving, he thumbed through his phone looking for an open restaurant where he could pick up a quick bite. When he found one, he put his phone away and grabbed the key to his motorcycle. He was about to start it and get the hell on the road, when he heard the scream and saw someone disappear behind the bar.

Immediately, he left the bike and ran around the back of the building where a trash bin and a vehicle occupied the dark alley. A man ran toward the vehicle, carrying something over his shoulder.

The trunk lid stood wide open.

His burden twisted and turned, and she cried out, "Put me down! Help! Help!"

Duff tensed and pushed off the ground, sprinting toward the man.

"Hey!" Duff yelled. "Let her go!"

"Help me!" the woman cried. She pushed against her captor's back, her face catching the limited light shining from a light over the back door of the bar.

Ivy.

Duff increased his pace, racing toward her.

The man leaned over the back of the trunk and dumped her in like a sack of potatoes.

She didn't stay still for long—her legs kicked out and she sat up, raising an arm to keep the trunk lid from smashing down on her head.

Her captor swung his fist, connecting with her face. She jerked back and sank into the trunk.

The man slammed the trunk lid down and turned to face Duff, a handgun pointing at Duff's chest.

Duff dove to the right as a shot rang out in the alley. He rolled to his feet and darted toward the heavy trash bin, using it for cover.

His heart raced and adrenaline pulsed through his veins. Unarmed, he was at a terrible disadvantage, but he couldn't let the man get away with Ivy in his trunk. He searched the area around the trash bin for anything he could use as a weapon.

He found a broken two-by-four with nails sticking out of it. Grabbing it, he looked around the corner of the trash bin.

When Ivy's captor yanked open the driver's door,

Duff made his move. He raced forward with the two-by-four and swung it hard before the man could aim properly.

The gun went off as the board hit the guy in the arm.

The bullet nicked Duff's thigh. He barely felt the sting, the adrenaline pumping through him carrying him forward. He balled his fists and swung hard, connecting with the man's chin. With his free hand, he gripped the man's wrist and directed the weapon away from his body.

"Drop it!"

The man fought for control of the gun while swinging his fist at Duff.

Duff ducked his head, receiving a glancing blow to his temple. He blinked and drove a right uppercut into the attacker's jaw.

His head snapped backward, and he staggered, falling against the car.

Duff held tight to the wrist of the hand holding the gun. It went off again, the bullet going wide of Duff's legs, hitting the pavement behind him. With a quick twist, he jerked the guy's arm up and slammed it against the car, knocking the gun loose. It clattered to the ground and skittered beneath the car.

Duff and the attacker struggled. Duff had the advantage of standing over the guy.

Then the man pushed away from his seat and hit

Duff in the gut with his shoulder, sending them both away from the car.

Now on relatively equal footing, Duff's hand-to-hand combat training kicked in. He twisted the man's arm around and spun him to face away, shoving the arm up between his shoulder blades.

The man kicked out behind him, catching Duff's ankle, making him loosen his hold to maintain his balance. He dove to the ground, jerking his hand free.

Before Duff could grab him, he rolled to the side, scrambled to his feet and ran into the shadows.

Duff started after him but stopped, afraid that if he went after the man, he'd circle back and get away with the car and the precious cargo in the trunk.

Duff ran back to the car and reached inside to trigger the latch release for the trunk. When the lid opened, he hurried around to the back.

Ivy sprang up and swung her fist, smashing it into Duff's jaw.

The blow stung, but Duff was pretty sure the force of her punch hurt her hand more than it hurt his face. "Hey, it's me."

She blinked several times, focused on his face, and raised her arms to him. "Oh, thank God."

He lifted her out of the trunk and held her close, his pulse only just beginning to slow as a residual tremor shook his body with the aftereffects of almost losing her to a thug.

"I didn't think I'd get to you in time," he admitted.

"I didn't think anyone would miss me until it was too late," she whispered, her breath warm against his neck. "Thank you."

He buried his face in her hair, his arms tightening around her. For a long moment, they remained locked in each other's embrace.

Duff would have held her even longer, but she spoke.

"Are you all right?" she asked.

"I should be asking that," he said, leaning back to peer at her face. "Looked like he hit you pretty hard."

She raised a hand to her temple where a lump and bruise were forming. "He did. I think he knocked me out. When I came to, it was dark. It took a moment for me to remember where I was. About that time, the trunk opened. I thought it was him coming back."

She looked up into his face. "I hit you pretty hard. Are you sure you're okay?"

He chuckled. "I've been hit harder. I'll live."

She cupped his cheek gently. "You're going to have a bruise."

"It'll match yours." He looked up. "We should call the police and report this incident. They might be able to trace the car and gather fingerprints."

She nodded but didn't move her cheek from where it lay against his chest. "I guess that means we have to go back inside."

"Or we could use my cellphone and call from here," he suggested.

"Yes, please. I don't want to cause a stir."

"Sweetheart, you didn't cause it. Whoever that was who attacked you did." He let her legs slide to the ground and held her with an arm around her waist, pressed against him while he pulled his cellphone from his back pocket and dialed 911.

After he reported the attack to dispatch, he brought up Merlin's number. "I'm going to let the guys know what happened. Are you okay with that?"

Ivy glanced around the back alley behind the bar and shivered. "The more the merrier, I always say. Or would it be closer to the truth to say there is safety in numbers?"

"Safety rules." He hit the call button and waited for Merlin to pick up.

"Miss us already?" Merlin answered.

"Need backup. Outside behind the bar. ASAP."

Merlin didn't question. "On it."

A moment later, the back door burst open and his team piled out.

"What happened?" Merlin asked.

Gwen appeared behind him. "Oh, dear God, Ivy!" She rushed toward her friend. "Are you okay?"

Ivy nodded. She didn't move out of the circle of Duff's arm. If anything, she leaned into him, and he liked it. "I'm okay. Thankfully, Magnus was here."

Duff explained what he'd seen and how he'd responded.

"Son of a bitch," Merlin muttered. "He might still be out there."

Immediately, they split up and searched the alley, going around the nearby buildings, bushes and shrubbery in yards close to the bar.

They returned, each shaking his head.

Merlin stood in the glow from the bulb over the back door of the bar. "Why would he go after Ivy?"

"Good question," Duff answered. "Could be a crime of convenience. Bastard could have been waiting for any female to exit the bar alone."

"I should have stayed outside watching until she got clean away," Merlin said. "I thought she would be all right since she was inside Gwen's car, all the windows rolled up. Hell, she was pulling out of the parking lot."

His team automatically turned, forming a perimeter around them. A siren blared, getting louder, heading to their location. Zip ran to the front of the building and directed the police and an ambulance to the rear where they waited.

The policemen questioned Ivy and Duff.

"The car was stolen," the policeman in charge of the scene said. "We'll take it to the impound lot and dust it for prints."

Emergency medical technicians checked Ivy and Duff. Ivy shook her head when they asked if she'd wanted them to take her to the hospital.

"We'll get her to the ER," Duff said.

"I don't need to go to the ER," Ivy insisted.

"Oh, honey." Gwen touched her arm. "You were knocked unconscious. You could have a concussion."

"I'll be fine."

Duff's arm around her waist tightened. "You're going."

She stiffened in his arms and frowned up at him. "You're not my boss or my mother."

"No, but you don't have a vehicle." He nodded as a couple of wreckers arrived.

"I could drive Gwen's car," she said. "It's only a broken window and seatbelt."

Duff shook his head.

"He's right, Ivy," Gwen said. "At the very least, let the ER doc decide if you're fine."

Ivy drew in a deep breath and let it out. "Okay."

"Merlin and I can take you," Gwen offered.

"I'm taking her," Duff announced.

Ivy leaned into him. "He saved my life. I trust him to get me there." Her brow puckered. "If it's not too much trouble."

"It's not." Duff's arm remained around her waist. So far, she hadn't objected, and he wasn't letting go. The image of the man hitting her and dumping her in the back of the car stuck with him, making his chest tighten.

He couldn't help thinking about what might have happened if he hadn't gotten to her fast enough. If he'd left before she'd been attacked.

The scenarios that could have been triggered those feelings of desperation he'd had when he'd tried to find Katie in the water after their boat capsized. He'd dived down numerous times, to no avail. He hadn't been able to save Katie, but he'd been there for Ivy.

He didn't want to let her go, afraid something else might happen to her if he did.

IVY HAD ALWAYS BEEN an independent woman, raised by a fiercely independent mother who knew her own mind, was educated and refused to bow down to any man, including her husband. Thankfully, Ivy's father knew what he was getting into and appreciated that his wife was strong and capable.

Because she'd grown up with a commanding mother who was insistent on the value of education, Ivy graduated high school at the top of her class. She went on to attain her undergraduate degree in three years—with honors—was accepted into law school, finishing and passing the bar the first time she took the test.

Working for one of the top law firms in Dallas, she'd been on the fast path to following her father and mother into politics.

Her law degree hadn't kept her client from being murdered by the man who'd raped her. The degree hadn't kept her attacker from throwing her into his trunk tonight. For that matter, it hadn't kept her from falling off the step ladder into the arms of a stranger. A dour-faced, sexy hulk of a stranger who'd saved her twice.

As independent as she'd always considered herself, she couldn't deny she felt safe in the curve of Duff's arm. She looked up at him, admiring his strength and the courage it took to run into battle, not away.

He glanced down at her, his gaze meeting hers. "Ready?"

She nodded.

"We can follow," Gwen said.

"No need," Ivy said. "I'm just going to have the doctor tell me what I already know. I'm fine." She hugged Gwen. "I'm sorry about your car."

Gwen snorted. "My car is the last thing I'm worried about. I'm more concerned about you."

"I don't like that the man got away," Merlin said.

"I'd have followed him, but that would've left Ivy alone and exposed if he'd doubled back."

Merlin laid a hand on Duff's shoulder. "You did the right thing. I'm just worried that he's still out there and might attack another woman."

Destiny nodded. "Hopefully, the fingerprints will help them locate him."

"If he has a prior arrest record," Ivy's lips thinned. "All too often, criminals get away with crimes until they're finally caught red-handed or caught for a lesser crime. Once they have their fingerprints on file, they're easier to identify at a crime scene."

Merlin tilted his head, his eyes narrowing slightly. "You sound like you know what you're talking about."

Gwen grinned. "Ivy was a prosecuting attorney."

Duff frowned down at her. "Was?"

Ivy looked away. "Was. I own a gift shop now."

"Less stress?" Destiny asked.

Ivy nodded and winced at the pain that shot through her temple. "Much less." *And less guilt at my own ineffectiveness.* She brushed her fingers over the bump near her eye.

"We're going to the hospital now," Duff said. Guiding her around the side of the building, he came to an abrupt halt as they emerged in the front parking lot. "Damn."

"What's wrong?" Ivy leaned into him.

"All I have is my motorcycle."

Zip handed him the keys to his Corvette. "Take my car. I'll ride your bike."

"Thanks, man," Duff said.

"We can switch off in the morning," Zip said. "Although, I might decide I like it a little too much and keep it."

"Whatever," Duff said.

Zip stared at Duff as if he'd grown a horn in the middle of his forehead. "Seriously? You're letting me drive your motorcycle?"

"I could act as shocked. You never let anyone else drive your Corvette."

"Yeah, well, these are special circumstances." Zip winked at Ivy. "Duff on a date doesn't happen every day."

"We're not on a date," Duff grumbled. "I'm taking the woman to the damned hospital."

"Which any one of us could do," Jangles pointed out.

Ivy's cheeks heated. "You don't have to take me," she said. He was getting enough grief from his friends. "I could go with Gwen and Merlin."

"I'm taking you," he said, his tone firm. Final. "The keys to my motorcycle are in the ignition. Helmet's on the seat." He marched forward, stopping in front of a shiny, sleek black Corvette.

Ivy gulped. "We're going in this? The way my luck is running, aren't you afraid we'll scratch it, or worse?"

"That's what insurance is for," Zip said behind them. "Go on. I'm looking forward to my bike ride."

Duff clicked the button to unlock the doors and held the passenger side open for Ivy, handling her with care.

Ivy sank into the leather seat and leaned her head back against the headrest.

Duff folded himself into the driver's seat, his big body taking up all the space. His knees bumped into the steering wheel. Duff muttered a single curse and slid the seat back a couple of inches.

Ivy's lips twitched, but she refrained from laughing. She could tell the man was uncomfortable in the confines of the sports car. "We could have gone on your bike."

He frowned. "No. You were knocked out. I couldn't risk it. And your dress." He lifted his chin toward her.

She smoothed a hand over the long skirt that would have been a hazard had it gotten caught in the motorcycle's spinning rear wheel. "Good point."

Duff drove to the hospital in silence.

Ivy honored his silence while a thousand questions filled her head. A head that was still spinning a little.

There weren't many people at the ER, so getting to the doctor didn't take as long as Ivy thought it would.

He checked her out and ran her through a CT scan. His verdict was that she might have a mild concussion, but that she could go home as long as someone watched her through the night for any changes. It wasn't necessary, but if she felt more comfortable, she could have that someone wake her every four hours to make sure she wasn't experiencing other symptoms like blurred vision, nausea, headache, ringing in the ears, or vomiting.

He looked to Duff. "Will you be staying with her?"

Ivy was shaking her head when Duff answered, "Yes, sir."

"Good. Call 911 if she has any of those symptoms."

"Yes, sir," Duff said.

As soon as she was discharged and they'd exited the hospital, Ivy turned to Duff. "You don't have to stay with me. I'll be fine. I don't have any of those symptoms."

"I'm staying. The question is, my place or yours?" He cocked an eyebrow in challenge.

Her eyes narrowed. "You're not budging on this, are you?"

"No, ma'am."

Too tired and emotionally drained to argue, she turned toward the car. "Mine." She'd figure out what to do with the man once they got there. A shiver of excitement rippled across her skin and heat built low in her belly.

She had to remind herself that he hadn't been interested in her as evidenced when he walked out of the bar without an explanation or a *fuck you*. That hadn't changed. He must be feeling some sense of responsibility for her to make him insist on staying with her.

He held the door for her as she dropped down into the Corvette.

"You know you're not responsible for me, right?"

she said, looking up at him. "I could catch a ride home and you don't have to be bothered."

He closed the door without commenting.

When he slid in beside her, she frowned. "You really don't talk much, do you?"

"No, ma'am."

"Look," she said, her frown deepening. "If you're going to stay the night at my house, you have to stop calling me ma'am."

CHAPTER 5

After Ivy gave Duff her address, she sat back in her seat and closed her eyes.

Duff drove highway 190 west from Killeen to Copperas Cove and turned off the main road into a subdivision of nice homes, many of them constructed of the white limestone prevalent in the area. He stopped in front of a one-story home with a rambling front porch with thick cedar posts.

The house was in a gated community with nice, well-maintained yards and two- or three-car garages attached to every home.

Duff didn't spend a lot of money and had a significant amount saved since he didn't have a family or expensive hobbies. He rode motorcycles, but he usually rebuilt them, rather than buying new.

It gave him great pleasure to work with his hands, lovingly restoring bikes that had been ill-treated or neglected for years. He usually sold them once he restored them to their former glory and usefulness. Still, he owned four he kept in his garage, alongside his black Toyota 4Runner.

Thinking about his 4Runner, he realized he'd subconsciously chosen his motorcycle, knowing it would be difficult to offer a ride home to a woman if she wasn't willing to ride on the back seat of his motorcycle. A good excuse not to offer.

Hindsight being what it was, Duff wished he'd brought his SUV. It was much more comfortable than Zip's Corvette and easier to get into and out of, especially if one was concussed and shaky from an encounter with a thug.

Duff parked in front of the garage, got out, and rounded to the passenger side where Ivy had pushed open the car's door.

Duff opened the door the rest of the way and reached out a hand to Ivy.

She took his hand and let him pull her out of her seat and onto her feet.

Ivy's knees buckled and she would have fallen except Duff caught her up against him and held her until she steadied.

"I don't know what's wrong with me," Ivy said. "I'm not normally this clumsy."

"You were attacked," Duff said.

"Hours ago," she argued. 'I shouldn't still be shaking."

"How many times in your life have you been attacked?"

"Counting tonight?" Ivy grimaced. "One."

"The first time leaves you a little in shock."

"I guess, being a Delta Force guy, you've been attacked numerous times." She leaned into him as he walked her to her front door.

"A few," he responded, liking the feel of her body against his a little more than he should for having only encountered her two times.

"Do you ever get used to being attacked?"

He shrugged. "I wouldn't say used to it, but you get a little hardened to it. You have a security system?"

"I turned it off from my phone when we pulled up." She pulled her keys out of her purse.

"Want me to do it?" he asked.

With a nod, she handed him the set and waited while he unlocked her door and pushed it inward.

Before she could step across the threshold, he stilled her with a hand on her arm. "Mind if I check the premises before you go inside?"

She frowned. "You think the attacker would be here? How would he know where I lived? He didn't get my purse."

Again, he shrugged. "I'd feel better clearing the building before you enter."

She waved a hand. "Have at it."

He stepped inside, flipped the light switch on the

wall, and looked into the rooms closest to the door before turning back to her and pulling her inside. "Wait in the front foyer while I clear the building."

He closed the door behind her and made a quick sweep of her home, looking for bad guys. Unarmed, he was careful to ease into rooms without exposing too much of his body to a potential gunman.

The house was empty except for Ivy's possessions —light and bright-colored furniture and paintings. Huge picture windows looked out over a dark backyard.

"All clear," he said and nodded toward the dark windows. "You might consider curtains or blinds. Anyone can look in and see you before you see them at night."

"I like my windows open. And my backyard is fenced. No one should be going back there without my permission."

"You give your permission for that guy to throw you in the trunk?" Duff asked.

Ivy's lips pressed into a thin line. "No. But I can't live in fear of someone always looking in my windows. I like light and sunshine."

"I'm not saying you should give up the light and sunshine. Just get some shades or curtains to cover them at night. You can't see out, but I guarantee, people can see in."

When she opened her mouth to argue, he held up his hand. "Your life. Your decision."

She nodded. "Right." She moved past him into a short hallway. Three bedrooms led off the hallway, a master and two guest bedrooms, one of which had been converted into an office with bookshelves lining the walls. As he'd passed the shelves, Duff had noted some impressive leather-bound volumes of law books.

Not only was she beautiful... she was smart. Smarter than he could ever hope or want to be. At least where laws were concerned. The book he bought at Gwen's shop on rebuilding engines was more in his lane. He liked working in tandem with his mind and hands. Nothing made him feel better than to take something that didn't work, that was ragged and dented, and bring it back to life and its original beauty.

Ivy led the way to one of the guest bedrooms. "You can sleep in here tonight. She smiled at the soft blues and whites. "It's not very masculine, but the bed is comfortable, and the sheets are clean."

Duff shook his head. "I'll sleep in the living room."

"The sofa isn't long enough for you," Ivy argued.

Duff snorted. "This bed isn't either. The sofa will be fine."

"Okay." She crossed the hallway to a linen closet and paused. "Sheet?"

"No," he said.

"Blanket?"

"No."

She frowned.

"Pillow?" he asked.

Ivy smiled, headed into the guest bedroom, pulled a pillow off the bed and handed it to him, shaking her head. "You're a hard one to read, did you know that?"

"I'm a simple man. I don't require much."

"I was raised to make guests feel at home," she said.

"I sleep on the ground beneath the stars or in my lounge chair at my place."

Ivy tilted her head. "I don't think I've ever slept on the ground beneath the stars. On a floor, yes, when I was a girl at a slumber party, but not outside, looking up at the stars."

Duff frowned. "You've never been camping?"

She shook her head. "No. My parents were politicians. They didn't have time to take me camping or hiking. While other kids were doing things like that, I was accompanying my parents to rallies and townhalls."

Ivy Fremont.

"Isn't there a senator Fremont from Texas?" Duff asked. "A female senator?"

A half-smile lifted Ivy's lips but never quite made it to her eyes. "Elizabeth Fremont."

"You related?"

"She's my mother."

Duff digested that piece of information. "And your father?"

"The late governor John Fremont."

"That's why you went into law?" he asked.

She nodded.

"Gwen told Merlin you were a store owner."

"I am. I quit the law firm and opened my own gift shop."

"Quit law?" He shook his head. "After all the effort it took to get your degree?"

She looked to the side. "It wasn't me."

"Why not?' You obviously have the intelligence."

"Sure. I'm smart enough to read, comprehend, and score high enough on tests. I was in criminal law. I watched too many bad guys get caught, go in front of a judge and get off on some technicality, only to go on to commit more and even worse crimes."

When she started to pass him in the hallway, he reached out and gripped her arm. "Did you lose one of those cases?"

Her lips twisted for a moment. "Yeah."

"He go on to commit more crimes?"

She nodded, a single tear slipping over the rim of her lower eyelid. "He killed the woman who testified against him."

"You felt like you hadn't done enough to put the bastard away." It was a statement. Duff knew what it felt like. He'd felt like he hadn't done enough to save Katie. He hadn't dived deep enough, long enough, or in the right place to find her in time to save her from drowning.

"I tried," she said, looking up at him with those emerald green eyes. No tears, just a hollowness that echoed in his own heart. "It wasn't enough."

Duff pulled her into his arms and held her. She wrapped her arms around his waist and laid her cheek on his chest.

For a long moment, they stood in the hallway, arms locked around each other.

Somewhere in the house a clock chimed, bringing Duff back to reality. He leaned back and brushed a strand of her hair back behind her ear. "You should get some sleep."

She nodded. "You, too."

For another long moment, they stood as if unwilling to break the bond formed in that one embrace.

Finally, Duff stepped backward and let his hands fall to his sides. He wanted to keep holding her. He reminded himself they were strangers, not lovers, and he was only there to make sure she didn't suffer any ill effects from the concussion.

He tilted her chin and stared at the lump at her temple.

"Will I have a shiner?" she asked.

He shook his head. "No. Just a bruise and a small goose-egg-sized bump."

"Seems like a lot of fuss for a little bump."

"Would be, if you hadn't been knocked unconscious." He brushed his thumb lightly across her cheek, touched her arm, and nodded his head toward the master bedroom. "Go." He needed her to go before he pulled her back into his arms and kissed her...like she'd kissed him in the bookstore. His gaze dropped to her lush lips. "Why?" he asked before he could think better of it.

Her brow creased. "Why what?"

"Why'd you kiss me in Gwen's bookstore?"

Her cheeks reddened and she looked away. "I don't know... It just...happened." Ivy looked up into his eyes.

Then he was pulling her into his arms, kissing her.

She ran her hands up his chest and around the back of his neck, dragging him closer, deepening another kiss that shouldn't have happened.

When at last they broke apart, Duff's breath was ragged, and his heart pounded against his ribs.

Ivy's chest rose and fell. She raised a hand to her mouth and stared at him, her eyes wide. "See? That's why I kissed you. I had to."

He chuckled, though it was difficult to do when he couldn't quite catch his breath. "Go to bed, Ivy, before I do it again."

She hesitated.

"Go," he repeated.

Ivy turned and ran into the master bedroom, closing the door behind her.

Duff drew in a deep, calming breath and let it out

slowly. What was it about the auburn-haired beauty that made him want more out of life than what he had?

He shook his head to clear his thoughts, squared his shoulders and retrieved the pillow from where it had fallen at his feet. When had that happened? Why couldn't he remember?

The woman filled his mind as he settled on the couch in the living room. He studied the paintings of gardens full of colorful flowers and sidewalk cafes with even more colorful flowers cascading over the edges of balconies.

What a stark contrast between this room and the office with all the bound leather tomes of law.

The woman dressed like a hippie from the seventies yet had the law degree to prove her intelligence and that she could hold her own in an argument or in court.

But no matter how smart she was, she hadn't had the strength to resist being kidnapped and thrown into a trunk.

Duff's hands clenched into fists. He hoped the police pulled some prints and they nailed the guy before he hurt someone else.

Especially not someone like Ivy.

IVY STOOD on the other side of her bedroom door for a long time, her heart beating so fast she felt as if she'd been running a marathon. And all she'd done was kiss a man. Only, he'd initiated it this time.

What did it mean?

Anything?

She was being ridiculous. They'd only really met that night. How could she be so consumed by him already?

Squaring her shoulders, she marched to her dresser and extracted clean panties and pajamas. Ivy put them back in the drawer and selected lacy panties and a silky baby doll nightgown. It wasn't like Duff would see them, but if the house caught on fire and he had to carry her out...

Before she could change her mind again, she hurried into the adjoining bathroom, turned on the water, stripped and studied her body, looking for any other bruises.

She had one on her hip and one on her right knee, as well as a bruise on her left upper arm.

Considering she had survived what could have been the last day of her life, she was okay with the war wounds.

Ivy stepped into the shower and let the warm water run over her head and body, letting it relax her and wash away the smell of the trunk she'd been locked in.

Lathering her hair, she released her worries and let them be sucked down the drain. At least she hoped the fear would go with the suds.

Never in her life had she been accosted and forced into a trunk. As the daughter of a governor and a senator, she'd never had anyone try to take her. Even working as a criminal lawyer, she'd never been threatened or stalked. Yes, she'd been yelled at in court, but she'd never felt like she had to watch her back.

She lived in a gated community, had a security system on her home and locked her car doors when she got in. How had she let herself become subdued so quickly and easily?

Shivering beneath the warm spray, she rinsed quickly, applied conditioner to her hair and rinsed again. When she turned off the water and reached for a towel, she thought again about the man in the other part of the house.

The kiss had been so good, how would it feel to have his mouth on other parts of her body?

The shiver of fear was replaced by a shiver of something else. Something warmer than the shower. The heat radiated from deep in her core, to swell in her chest and rise up her neck into her cheeks.

Ivy rubbed the towel over her skin, wondering how it would feel to have Duff dry her from head to toe.

What am I thinking? The man had run out of the bar like his hair was on fire.

Then he'd kissed her.

The man blew hot then cold then hot again.

What was his problem? Had he been in a bad relationship? Was that what made him run?

Ivy sighed. It didn't matter. He was only there for the night. And only to make sure she didn't die of an aneurism or swelling on the brain. After that, they wouldn't see each other again.

Unless he asked her out on a date. The likelihood of that was pretty slim.

Ivy brushed the tangles out of her hair and dressed in the panties and minuscule nightgown, loving the way the silky material slid across her naked skin. Again, all thoughts went to the man lying on the couch in her living room. Would he like the way she dressed?

She crawled between her sheets and lay her head down on her pillow. Never had her bed felt so empty before.

She thought of the pillow she'd given to Duff. Was he using it? Her gaze went to the empty pillow beside her.

If he really wanted to make sure she was okay all night, wouldn't it be better if he slept in the same room with her?

How would he feel if she asked him to sleep in her room? In her bed? With her?

Butterflies fluttered inside her belly and her core heated all over again.

Sleep, you idiot. He's not that into you.

Ivy closed her eyes and willed her pulse to slow,

her breathing to deepen and sleep to claim her.

After twenty minutes of deep breathing, she still wasn't sleepy.

She hadn't had dinner. A snack and a drink might help. For that matter, maybe Duff was hungry, too.

Swinging her legs over the side of the bed, she rose, wrapped the robe that matched her nightgown around her, and stepped out into the hallway. The cool draft of the air conditioner reminded her of just how short the nightgown and robe were.

She shrugged. Her legs were her best asset. What would it hurt to show them off?

Ivy tiptoed barefoot down the hallway and across the living room.

Duff lay on the sofa, his eyes closed, starlight bathing him in a deep blue glow.

Ivy's breath caught in her throat and she stopped mid-stride.

The man was ruggedly gorgeous, his broad shoulders wider than the cushions on the couch. He'd slipped off his boots. His socked feet hung over the arm of the sofa. With his arms crossed over his chest, he appeared to be sound asleep.

Ivy turned to complete her trek to the kitchen.

"Are you feeling all right?" His voice stopped her in place.

She spun to face him, drawing the edges of her robe closer around her. "Y-yes."

"Not thinking about the bastard who attacked you?" He opened one eye and then the other.

Her pulse kicked up a notch. "Some."

"He won't get to you here."

"Are you sure?"

He sat up and swung his legs to the ground. "Positive." He tipped his chin toward the kitchen. "Hungry?"

"I am. I don't think I had dinner."

"Me either. Want to go out for something?"

She grinned and drew her robe around herself even tighter. "Not dressed for that."

His gaze swept over her attire, lingering on the hem and the long expanse of legs beneath. "No. You're not. What have you got here? Do you want me to cook something?"

She cocked a brow. "You can cook?"

"I'm a bachelor. It's cook, eat out or starve. "I get tired of eating out and you can tell I don't starve."

Oh, she could tell he didn't starve. He was built, muscular and strong, his arms and chest stretching the T-shirt he wore...deliciously.

Duff looked past her to the kitchen. "What have you got?"

"I have a rotisserie chicken in the refrigerator," she said. "We can slice it up and make sandwiches."

"Tortillas?" he asked.

"Flour," she responded. "Why?"

"Cheese and salsa?"

74

Ivy nodded.

"I make a mean chicken quesadilla," Duff said.

"Mmm. I'll get out the pan," Ivy said. "The ingredients are in the fridge."

They worked together to debone the chicken, cut up a salad, and cook the quesadillas. When all was ready, they carried their plates to the bar.

They slathered the quesadillas in salsa and consumed them with little talking between them.

When her plate was clean, Ivy sat back and rubbed her tummy. "Wow, that was really good."

"Told you," he said, gathering her plate. "Cook or starve."

"I usually settle for a salad," Ivy said. "This was so much better."

"Glad you liked it."

She hopped up and went to her stash of alcohol, selecting a bottle of her favorite wine. "Care to join me?"

After setting their plates in the sink, Duff turned. "Sure." He returned to the bar and sat beside her.

Ivy set a bottle of wine between them with a corkscrew.

Duff opened the bottle, poured two glasses, and handed one to her. The other, he lifted. "To narrow escapes."

She touched her glass to his. "To narrow escapes."

They each drank.

Ivy held up her glass. "To perfect timing." She

smiled. "If you had taken off as soon as you'd left the bar, we wouldn't be sitting here now."

His lips pressed together. "I'm glad I was still there."

"Why didn't you leave right away? Did you have trouble with your motorcycle?"

His mouth twisted. "I was having second thoughts about leaving the bar." He looked across his glass of wine, his gaze capturing hers. "And you."

Her eyes widened. "Why did you leave the bar so fast? Did I say something stupid? I thought we were getting along pretty well."

"We were getting along great."

Her brow sank. "Then why did you leave?"

"I wasn't ready for us to get along so well."

"Not ready?" She set her glass on the bar and touched his arm. "I don't mean to be nosy. I just want to understand."

"I liked dancing with you," he said.

"So, you ran out of the bar?"

"I liked it too much." He stared at his glass of wine.

"That doesn't make sense," she said.

"And I liked our kiss in the bookstore." Still staring in the glass.

"Then why did you leave?" she asked.

He looked up into her eyes. "I felt guilty."

Guilty?" her frown deepened. "For what?"

"That I was enjoying my time with you. And you weren't Katie."

Her heart sank to her knees. "Katie?" she whispered.

He nodded. "My wife."

Ivy leaned back in her chair. "You're married?" Her gut knotted around the food she'd just consumed.

His face seemed to darken. "I was."

The knot loosened a little. "Divorced?"

"Widowed."

"Oh." Ivy shook her head. "I'm sorry."

"We'd been married three days when she died."

Ivy's heart sank again. This time for Duff. "On your honeymoon?"

"Yes."

"I'm sorry, Duff." She laid her hand on his arm.

"It's been eight years," he said. "You'd think I'd have moved on."

"You must have loved her so very much."

He nodded. "We were so young. Thought we were invincible. Until the chartered fishing boat capsized. I lost my hold on her when the boat flipped. There was a lot of confusion, and debris floating in the water. Everyone came up but Katie."

"I'm so sorry. What a nightmare." Ivy didn't know what else to say. She poured more wine and lifted her glass. "To Katie," she said.

He touched his glass to hers. "Katie."

No wonder he'd left the bar in such a hurry.

Ivy drank her glass of wine. Resigned.

Duff would never be interested in her. Not like Katie. Ivy wouldn't even compete with her ghost.

Duff was still in love with his dead wife.

CHAPTER 6

Duff downed his glass of wine and stood. "We should get some rest."

"Yes. We should," Ivy responded, her tone flat, her lips pressed together. "Thank you for cooking dinner."

"You're welcome," he said.

"Leave the dishes in the sink. I'll clean up in the morning."

He nodded and set their wine glasses on the counter beside the sink. "Good night, Ivy," he said.

"Good night, Magnus." She turned and padded down the hall in her bare feet.

Duff swallowed a groan.

The woman had legs. Long, shapely legs that could wrap around a man's waist and hold him close as he pumped his seed into her.

The nightgown and robe combination wasn't helping his focus.

He was there to make sure she didn't have a concussion, not to make love to her.

His groin tightened. Oh, but he wanted her. So much so, his body ached.

In the living room, he stood in the dark, staring out the huge picture windows into the starlit Texas sky.

Was he ready to start dating? Would Ivy go out with him, if he asked? After he'd ditched her in the Ugly Mug would she trust him to show up at her door to take her to a nice dinner or on a picnic? Or should he cut his losses and go back to his motorcycles and cooking meals for himself?

Yes, Ivy had awakened something in him. Her kisses made him want more.

Knowing she was lying in a bed down the hallway, in her sexy nightgown, her naked legs sliding across the sheets...

If she showed any signs of interest in the morning, he would apologize for running out of the bar. Then he'd ask her to take a chance on him and go out with him.

He liked her. She was smart, beautiful, and strong. It took that kind of woman to be with a Delta Force soldier.

His mind made up, he stretched out on the couch,

tucked his hands behind his head, and stared up at the ceiling.

And stared. And stared.

He must have fallen asleep because he woke to the sound of a muffled scream.

Duff rolled off the couch and onto his feet. It took a split second for him to remember where he was and which direction he needed to run.

He ran down the hallway to the master bedroom and burst through the door, slapping on the light.

Ivy sat up in her bed, her eyes wide, her cheeks wet from tears. "Magnus?"

His gaze swept the room, searching for the danger. When he realized it was empty but for her, he relaxed and crossed to the bed. "Are you all right? No pain or dizziness?"

She nodded. "I'm okay. Why are you here?"

"I thought I heard a scream." He reached out and brushed a tear from her cheek. "Are you sure you're all right?"

She nodded. "I was having a dream."

"More like a nightmare." He brushed another tear from her other cheek.

Ivy leaned into his hand. "He caught me and carried me away from the bar. I fought, but I couldn't get away."

Duff lowered himself to sit on the side of her bed. "Do you want me to stay until you go back to sleep?"

Ivy bit her bottom lip. "I'm not usually so clingy."

"I won't tell anyone if you don't."

"Then, yes." Ivy scooted over to the other side of the bed. "Please, stay."

"Until you go to sleep." He laid on the bed beside her, wondering if he was about to make a very big mistake.

As soon as he was settled, she reached for his hand. "I'm sure I'll be fine in the morning. She raised his hand and tucked it between her cheek and the pillow. "Thank you."

For a long time, he lay holding his breath, willing his pulse to slow, his body to relax and sleep.

It wasn't happening.

Ivy's eyes closed and her breathing grew deep and regular. She rolled toward him and draped her other arm over his chest and her calf over his.

Duff muffled his groan and held onto his desire by a thread. After a while, he couldn't take it anymore. He either had to get the hell out of her bedroom or make love to her.

He eased one leg over the side of the bed and then lifted her wrist and positioned her arm over the curve of her waist and hip. His knuckles brushed across the silky fabric of her nightgown and he nearly came undone.

Steeling himself against his natural instincts, he scooted to the edge of the bed intending to roll off onto the floor.

Ivy drew in a deep breath and reached for him

again, laying her arm over his chest, her hand circling the back of his neck. "Don't go," she whispered into his ear.

"Sweetheart, if I don't go, I can't be held responsible for my actions."

"Please," she said. "I want you."

His breath caught and held as he looked down to find that her eyes were open, and she was staring up into his. "Are you awake?"

She nodded and stretched. The leg that had been slung across his returned to slide over his shin and up to his thigh. "Stay."

He hesitated. "Do you know what you're asking?"

She nodded. "Do you have protection?"

His heartbeat sped up. "Yes."

"Hold me?" she said, her tone a question. "If you want to, that is."

"Oh, sweetheart," he said, pulling her into his arms. "I want to. I just don't want you to regret it in the morning." He pressed a kiss to her forehead, careful not to bump the knot at her temple.

"I'll regret it if we don't."

She lifted her chin, offering her mouth to him.

He took it, gently at first, his lips moving over hers, feeling his way.

When she opened to him, he dove deeper, sliding his tongue across hers.

She wove her fingers into the hair at the back of his neck and pressed her breasts against his chest.

Duff's groin tightened, his erection hardening against her soft belly. He leaned back. "We barely know each other."

"Doesn't that make it even more exciting?" she whispered and brushed her lips against the base of his neck where his pulse pounded. "Don't worry. I have no expectations for the morning. I won't demand to see you again. I just want tonight."

What if he wanted more?

She leaned up and brushed her lips across his. "You feel it, don't you? Or is it only me?"

He crushed his lips to hers in a kiss that rocked him to his very soul. When he came up for air, he leaned his forehead against hers. "I feel it, too."

She sighed, a smile parting her lips. Her auburn hair fanned out across the white pillowcase, creating a beautiful backdrop for her pale skin and green eyes.

"You are beautiful," he said and kissed her lightly, his lips trailing across her cheek and down over her chin and the long line of her graceful neck. He didn't stop until he came to where the strap of her nightgown crossed her collarbone.

He looked up to capture her gaze.

She nodded at his unspoken question.

Duff slipped the strap off her shoulder and pressed a kiss to her collarbone. He blazed a path down to the swell of her right breast beneath the silky fabric.

Ivy touched a finger beneath his chin and brought

him back to her lips for a brief kiss. Then she sat up, hooked the hem of her gown in her fingers and whipped it up over her head, letting it drop silently to the floor.

Duff leaned up on an elbow and swept her body with his gaze, his heart hammering in his chest, his blood burning in his veins.

She reached for his T-shirt and tugged it free of his jeans.

He brushed her hands aside and ripped his shirt off, tossing it to the corner. Then he leaned over her, his hands on either side of her head. "Just say the word and I'll stop."

"Are you insane? There's no stopping now." She wound her arms around his neck and dragged his head down to her, pressing her mouth to his.

He plundered and ravaged her lips, nibbling at their fullness and sucking her tongue between his teeth. Duff quickly shifted lower, anxious to taste all of her. He captured one of her rosy-tipped breasts between his lips and sucked it in, pulling hard.

She arched her back, pressing her breast deeper into his mouth.

He took it, laving and nipping at the beaded tip until Ivy moaned and writhed beneath him.

Then he transferred his attention to the other breast and treated it to the same.

Ivy's fingers wove into his hair and pressed into his scalp.

He slipped lower, kissing and tonguing each rib, passing over her bellybutton to stop at the elastic of her sexy lace panties.

He hooked his thumbs into the band and dragged them downward, exposing the tuft of coppery hair covering her sex.

She stilled beneath him, her breath arrested, her body waiting for his next move.

Duff blew a warm stream of air over her mons and pushed to his feet.

Ivy gasped. "What's wrong?"

He chuckled. "I'm overdressed." He quickly rectified the problem, stripping out of his boots and jeans. When he came back to her, he hooked her legs in his arms and dragged her toward the edge of the bed.

Ivy squeaked. "Hey."

He dragged her panties down to her ankles and let them fall to the floor, then he dangled her legs over the edge of the bed and parted her knees.

Ivy leaned up on her elbows. "What..."

"Shh," he said, pressing a finger to her lips. "Trust me?"

"I don't know you," she said, her eyes wide.

His lips curved upward. "That makes it even more exciting, right?"

She nodded slowly, her eyes still wide.

Duff dropped to his knees, draped her legs over his shoulders and parted her folds with his thumbs. "I'm just getting to know you," he said and flicked his tongue over that little nubbin of flesh he knew to be packed with a fine array of nerves designed to stimulate her entire body.

Ivy stiffened, her toes curling upward. "Oooo... yessss..." she moaned.

With the very tip of his tongue, he flicked her again.

Her fingers dug into his scalp and pulled hard on his hair. It didn't hurt so much as make him even harder.

Duff settled into a rhythm of tonguing, laving and flicking her clit until she thrashed against the comforter, her hips rising with every touch until she froze. Her hands spasmed in his hair, pushing and pulling in a frenetic dance.

He continued his campaign until her hands slammed down on the mattress and she rose to meet his mouth, her hips pulsing with her release.

When she finally relaxed against the mattress, he scooted her up in the bed and lay down between her legs. He leaned over the side, grabbed his jeans, fished out his wallet, and secured two foil packets. One, he placed on the nightstand, the other, he tore open and rolled down over his engorged cock.

Ivy lifted her knees, clutched his hips and guided him to her core.

He nudged her entrance. "Still with me?"

"For someone who is usually quiet, you talk a lot," she said. "Shut up and make love to me."

He chuckled. "As you wish." He eased into her slick channel.

Ivy curved her fingers around his ass and slammed him home. "Ahhh...that's more like it."

"In a hurry to get somewhere?" he asked.

"Yes. To get you inside me. All. The. Way." She wrapped her legs around his waist and dug her heels into his lower back. "I need you, Magnus. Don't stop. Don't slow down. Make magic."

He pumped in and out of her, moving faster and faster, his body tensing, blood rushing through his veins and down to his manhood.

When he reached the point of no return, he launched over the edge, slammed into her once more and held his position as he milked his release to the very last quiver.

As he fell back to earth, he dropped down onto Ivy and lay for a moment, loving the feel of her skin against his, their connection still real and tight. Then he wrapped his arms around her and rolled over on his side, taking her with him.

Ivy rested her cheek against his chest, a sigh escaping her lips "Amazing," she whispered.

"Agreed." He pressed his forehead to hers. "Now, sleep."

"How can I after that?" she said.

"Close your eyes." He bent and pressed a kiss to each eyelid. "You'll be asleep before you know it."

"Mmm. I doubt it." A yawn spread across her face,

belying her words. "Thank you," she whispered as she nestled in beside him.

"For what?"

"For saving my life." Ivy yawned, smothering it against his chest. "Twice." Her body relaxed against his, her breathing slowed.

"Thank you," Duff said softly. "For saving mine."

CHAPTER 7

IVY WOKE the next day to sun slashing across her face, prying at her eyelids. She frowned. Why was the sun shining through her window? Normally, she closed the blinds before she went to bed. Had she forgotten?

Then it hit her. She'd made love with a stranger last night.

Her eyes opened wide and she turned to the pillow beside her.

It was empty.

Had she imagined making love with Duff? She ran her hands over her chest and down her torso, taking stock of her body. There was no denying the ache between her legs and the beard burn across her breasts. Yes. She'd been thoroughly fucked. And it felt wonderful.

She kicked off the sheets and stretched her arms and legs, loving the feel of the cool air across her skin. Her gaze went to the adjoining bathroom. Was he in there, doing his morning ablutions? Would he walk in and find her lying naked and exposed on the mattress and make love to her again?

Ivy strained to listen for movement or the sound of running water. When she heard neither, she sighed. Perhaps he was in the kitchen rummaging through her refrigerator, having worked up a huge appetite after all the work he'd done the night before, saving her and then giving her the best orgasm she'd had in...hell, forever.

She swung her legs over the side of the bed and stood, still hoping he would come into the room and pick up where they'd left off when she'd fallen asleep. Another sigh and she slipped her semi-sheer robe over her naked body, hurried into the bathroom to relieve herself and brush her hair and teeth.

When she was finished, she left her bedroom and padded down the hallway to the kitchen. Still no sign of Duff.

Disappointment rushed in to wipe away the sense of fulfillment she'd had after sex with Duff. But for him, that must have been all it was.

Sex.

He'd banged her and left.

Who was she kidding? She'd told him she would expect nothing in the morning. Otherwise, he might not have even touched her, much less made love to her.

Ivy leaned her forehead against the refrigerator, her chest tight, her heart hurting.

Hands gripped her shoulders and a deep, sexy voice said, "Hey. Are you all right?"

In a flash, Ivy went from totally depressed to over the moon. At only the sound of his voice. *Oh, man.* She was getting it bad, and only after a day of knowing him.

He turned her in his arms and pulled her against his chest. "What's wrong?"

She smiled up at him brightly. "Nothing, now that you're here."

He kissed her forehead. "How do you feel?"

Her cheeks heated. "Actually, pretty good."

"Considering you were tossed into the back of a car and knocked out." His lips twisted in a wry smile. "I'd say that's good."

She hadn't even thought about her encounter with the mugger. Her physical well-being had more to do with how her body felt following having been with him. She wound her arms around his waist. "How do you feel?" She frowned. "You didn't get much sleep."

"I don't require a lot," he said and pressed a kiss to her forehead. "How's the bump?"

"I don't feel it unless I touch it," she said. It was a good sign that he had his arms around her, wasn't it?

She was dying to ask him what his plans were for the day. After telling him she had no expectations of him, she didn't feel it was appropriate. If he wanted to extend their relationship from a one-night stand to something more, he'd have to make the next move.

He ran his hands over her shoulders and down her back, his irises flaring as his hands skimmed across her bottom. Then he lifted, backed her up to the counter and sat her on the edge.

She automatically parted her thighs to let him step between.

He nuzzled her neck. "You don't have on anything under that robe, do you?"

Her heart fluttered and she shook her head.

Duff lifted her chin and kissed her lips, sliding his mouth across them and down her neck to where the pulse beat so fast, she was sure it would leap out of her skin.

He parted the lapels of her robe and cupped each breast in his palms. Then he bent to take one in his mouth, tonguing it until it puckered into a tight little bead.

Ivy caressed the back of his head and guided him to the other nipple.

He nipped the tip and sucked it into his mouth, making all kinds of sensations erupt inside of her. The cool quartz countertop did nothing to chill the heat building at Ivy's core.

She reached for the button on his jeans and pushed it through the hole. Then she lowered the zipper.

His cock sprang free into her hand. "Still have that other condom?" she asked.

"I rescued it from the nightstand while I was getting dressed." He reached into his pocket and handed it to her.

She made quick work of tearing it open and sliding it down over his thick shaft, fondling his balls below. Then she scooted to the edge of the counter and guided him to her.

He paused, his erection pressing against her entrance. "What about foreplay?"

She shook her head. "At times like this, it's overrated."

He shook his head. "I don't think so."

He cupped her sex in the palm of his hand and slid a finger into her. He swirled inside her and then brought it out, covered in her juices. Then he parted her folds and applied the wet finger to her clit, stroking her until she squirmed.

"Okay," she said, her voice ragged with her growing desire. "You're right. Foreplay is never overrated." She flung back her head and braced her hands on the counter while he flicked his finger over that little strip of flesh, bringing her to the very edge.

Her breath caught and held in her chest as he moved into position and slid into her.

She held onto the counter as he thrust into her again and again, driving her over the edge.

The tingling started at her center and spread outward. She shuddered with the force of her release.

As Ivy rode the wave, Duff pumped several more times and then stiffened. "Sweet heaven," he muttered, as he thrust one last time, driving deep into her. He held her hips, crushing her to him, holding tightly as his cock pulsed against the walls of her channel.

She clung to him until the waves of sensations ebbed and she relaxed against him. "Wow."

"Yeah," he said. "Wow." Slowly, he slid out of her, removed the condom, tossed it into the garbage bin, and then reached into a drawer for kitchen towels. He handed one to her and used the other to clean up.

"I'd carry you back to your bedroom and do that all again, but I'd need a little recovery time and breakfast is ready."

She laughed, collected their towels, and stowed them in the laundry room beside the kitchen. "You've been busy."

"Yes, I have." He stepped back and waved a hand toward the kitchen table where he'd laid out two plates with flatware and a small plate filled with buttered toast. "I made scrambled eggs. They're keeping warm in the oven."

"You really do know how to cook." A smile curled her lips. She could easily get used to waking up to his face in the morning. And to making love on the kitchen counter. She'd designed the kitchen herself but making love on the cool quartz counters hadn't been part of her thought process. She considered it a happy bonus.

He wrapped her robe around her, tying the sash securely. "Reducing temptation," he murmured.

Then he held out a chair for her at the table. "Sit."

She laughed. "I'm not a dog." Still, she took the seat and let him wait on her.

He brought a pan full of fluffy yellow eggs, a platter of bacon and a pitcher of orange juice to the table.

After he filled her glass and his, he settled into the seat beside her. "Eat."

She smiled. "Thank you for breakfast," she said and scooped a spoonful of eggs onto her plate, selected a couple of pieces of bacon and a slice of toast.

Once Ivy was finished filling her plate, Duff followed suit.

The eggs were cooked to perfection and the bacon was crisp like she liked it. But the company was what made the meal amazing.

As she swallowed the last piece of toast she was about to commend him on his cooking skills when her cellphone emitted a hen's squawk, the sound she'd assigned to her mother's number.

The sunny day dimmed. She tried to ignore the noise, but years of answering when her mother called brought her to her feet. Besides, her mother had been ignoring her, and who knew when the woman would deign to call Ivy again?

"I'd better answer that. It's my mother."

His lips quirked.

"She's a force to be reckoned with," she said and hurried to dig her cellphone out of her purse and answer her mother's video call.

Her mother's face materialized on the screen. "Ivy, what took you so long to answer?"

Irritation rose in Ivy. "Mother, I could say the same. You didn't answer the previous times I called over the past two weeks, nor did you return my calls. You're lucky I decided to answer my phone."

"I've been busy," she stated, as if her busy trumped everything in anyone else's life.

"I have a life, too," Ivy said. "Yet, I make an effort to call you."

"Why is your hair such a mess and you're still in your nightclothes at this hour?" By contrast, her mother had her 'senator face' on.

"It's Saturday, Mother," Ivy said slowly. "I don't open the store until noon."

"When are you going to come to your senses and sell that store? I spoke with your old boss last week. He said he was holding a position for you at the firm."

"Not interested," Ivy said. "I'm done with law."

"You can't be serious."

Ivy's lips firmed. "As serious as a heart attack, Mother."

"Don't joke about heart attacks. Your father died of one."

"Exactly. That's how serious I am about not going back to the firm," Ivy said. "Now, change the subject or I end this call."

Her mother huffed. "I didn't call to cajole you into returning to the firm. Although, I would prefer that."

Ivy tensed, ready to call her own bluff and end the call.

"I called because I wanted to let you know that I've hired a new company to handle my personal security."

Ivy frowned. "What was wrong with the old one?"

"Not experienced enough. The new one has retired special operations personnel."

"As in Navy SEALs, Rangers and Delta Force?" Ivy's gaze went to Duff.

His eyebrows rose, but he didn't say anything.

"Precisely," her mother said.

"Why the specialty?" Ivy asked.

"I feel more comfortable knowing I'm protected by some of our country's finest."

Ivy frowned. "Is something going on that I need to know about?"

"No, dear. I just wanted to let you know there might be one more layer of security you might have to go through to get to me, should you decide to come to see me while I'm in Texas."

"And when will that be?"

"I'll be in Austin next Wednesday," she said.

"Good to know. I'll have to look at my calendar. I don't close the shop until five in the afternoon. If I come, it will have to be for dinner."

"Ivy, you know I'll be booked for official dinners," her mother said. "Can't you have one of your staff cover for you at the shop?"

"You know I'm a one-person shop. I'm doing it all myself," she said. Her mother would know that if she'd cared enough about her business to ask.

Behind her, Duff rose from his chair, collected the plates and carried them across the kitchen to the sink.

"Ivy Elaine Fremont," her mother started.

Ivy held her breath, ready for her mother's next barrage. "Yes, Mother?" She had to remind herself she hadn't heard from her mother in weeks and she shouldn't be short with her now.

"Who is that man in your house with you?"

Ivy winced inwardly. The last thing she wanted was for her mother to insert herself into her sex life. For all she knew, this was a one-night stand. Her mother didn't need to know anything about Duff.

"He's a friend," Ivy said, her cheeks heating.

"I can tell when you're lying. Are you seeing someone?"

"None of your business, Mother."

"It is if the press gets hold of you."

"Not my problem."

"Your problems are my problems," her mother said. "Everything you do is a reflection on me and any campaign I wish to run."

"I'm not the one running for reelection," Ivy pointed out. "And how I spend my weekends are my business, not yours."

"Young man," her mother raised her voice. "Young man."

Duff leaned over Ivy's shoulder. "Yes, ma'am?"

Ivy drew in a deep breath and let it out slowly, waiting for her mother to embarrass the crap out of her.

"Who are you and where do you work?" her mother demanded.

"Magnus McCormick, US Army."

Her mother's eyes narrowed. "MOS?

"Can't say. It's Top Secret."

Elizabeth Fremont's eyes widened. "Special Forces." She nodded. "Are you going to be around for long?"

Ivy winced. They hadn't discussed the future. She didn't even know if he'd ask her out again.

"It depends," Duff said, his breath warming the back of her neck.

"On what?" her mother wanted to know.

Ivy glared at the screen. Her thumb moved to hit

the end button on the video call.

"On whether your daughter will go out with me again."

Her thumb hovered over the button and her breath caught in her throat.

"And will you, Ivy?" Her mother was relentless.

"He hasn't asked," she said through gritted teeth.

"Mr. McCormick, do you intend to ask?"

Ivy swallowed hard on a mortified groan.

"I do, ma'am."

"Well then, what are you waiting for?" Elizabeth Fremont's well-maintained eyebrow cocked.

Duff's hands came up around Ivy's waist, out of her mother's view. "Will you go out with me?"

Heat burned through her where his arms wrapped around her middle. With him standing so close, she could barely breathe, much less concentrate on the conversation they were having with her mother, of all people. "Yes," she said. She didn't give a damn if her mother approved.

"Good," her mother said. "I'm glad to hear that. It's good to know my daughter will be well-protected."

Duff's arms tightened around Ivy. "Senator Fremont, should I be concerned about protection?"

"I don't think so, but just in case, it's good to know she'll have you around."

Ivy's gut clenched. "Mother, what are you not telling me?"

"Just that I'm concerned for my only daughter."

"Since when have you ever been concerned about me?" Ivy narrowed her eyes. "Other than to tell me how I should live my life."

"I told you. I've hired a better security company to protect me."

Ivy stiffened. "From what?"

The senator's eyes widened. "Didn't I tell you?"

Oh, no, she hadn't. Ivy braced herself. "Tell me what?"

"I've received several threatening messages. Nothing for you to worry about."

"If you're concerned for your safety and now mine, I'm worried," Ivy said.

Her mother sighed. "So far, the messages have only been directed toward me."

"Why would someone threaten you?" Ivy asked.

Her other hand brushed an imaginary hair away from her brow. "I'm leading a committee in charge of halting illegal gun sales to foreign governments. We think it has to do with the regulations I'm proposing to Congress."

Ivy shook her head. "New regulations are brought before Congress all the time. Since when do they come with threats? And by threats, I assume you mean death threats or threats to do bodily harm?"

"Have they identified where those threats are coming from?" Duff asked.

"Not yet. Just that I needed to beef up security and warn my family."

"Damn it, Mother, you never call and beat around the bushes. Why start now?"

"I wasn't sure if you would take it seriously." Her mother's brow furrowed, and all pretense left her senator face. "I'm worried about you, Ivy. We might not always see eye to eye, but you're my only daughter, and I really do care about you. I don't want anything to happen to you because of what I have to do for the country."

Ivy leaned back into the warmth and stability of Duff's chest. "Is it that bad?"

Her mother nodded. "It could be."

"Okay, I'll keep my guard up."

"And your man, Magnus? You'll keep him with you?"

"Mother, he has his job, I have mine. I can't rely on him to be around at all times. But I will watch my back and be sure to lock my doors and turn on my security system at night."

"I hope that will be enough. I was hoping you'd say Magnus was your lover and sleeping with you at night. My mind would be more at ease knowing you have a skilled combat soldier with you."

Ivy nearly choked on her shock and embarrassment. "Mother, please. Duff and I barely know each other."

"Well, what are you waiting for? Do you need me to hire some more men from the security firm I've gotten for myself to defend you?"

"No, Mother. I don't need anyone to defend me. I've got my conceal carry license. I'll carry a gun. I can take care of myself."

Her mother nodded. "Good. But it would help to have someone watching your back. You can't keep an eye out in all directions all the time. Perhaps you should close your shop for a couple of weeks until all of this settles down."

"I'm not closing my shop." Ivy squared her shoulders. "I need to get ready for work. Stay safe, Mother. And let me know if you get any more threats. Otherwise, I'll see you on Wednesday after I close the shop."

"You won't consider closing early?"

"No, Mother. I have set hours so people will know when I'm opened and closed and plan accordingly. I was taught that punctuality is the bedrock of discipline and a good moral character."

Her mother chuckled softly. "Touché, daughter. Touché."

Ivy's lips curved upward. "Later, Mother. Keep your bodyguards close and stay safe."

"You, too, Ivy. I might not tell you often enough, but I love you, and only want the best for you."

"I know, Mother. I love you, too." Ivy ended the call and turned to Duff.

For a long moment, they stared at each other.

Ivy broke the silence first. "Do you think the guy

who attacked me last night was someone who is trying to get to my mother?"

Duff shrugged. "I don't know. But it wouldn't hurt to find out who's threatening your mother and why."

"I'll text her later today and see if she's learned any more about the threats. For now, though, I need to get ready for work." Still, she didn't make a move to leave the kitchen.

"For the record, you don't have to ask me out, just because my mother wanted you to." She lifted her chin. "I'm really not a charity case. I can get a date without my mother intervening."

Duff's expression didn't change.

Ivy was having a hard time reading him.

"I don't say things out of convenience," he said, pulling her into his arms. "So?"

Ivy's heart fluttered. "So, what?"

"Go out with me?" he said.

"Don't let my mother guilt you into you taking me out." Ivy rested her hands on his chest. "I told you, no expectations."

Duff cocked an eyebrow. "You didn't answer my question."

"You didn't ask me out because you think I need protection, do you?"

"Everything aside...this is me," he covered her hands on his chest, "asking you."

The dour look he'd had on his face when she'd first met him had disappeared. He didn't have a smile. But he didn't look like he was mad or disappointed in the world.

"I just want you to know that I do have my conceal carry license and I own a gun," she said.

At that point, his lips twitched into the resemblance of a smile. "Should I be afraid?"

Her mouth quirked. "Maybe. I'm just letting you know that I can take care of myself."

"Got it," he said. "You still haven't answered my question."

She stared up into his eyes, looking for anything indicating her mother's conversation had influenced his decision to ask her out. When she didn't see anything, Ivy smiled. "Okay."

He nodded. "Should I pick you up at your shop?"

Her eyes rounded. "Tonight?"

"Did I not make myself clear?" he said. "Is tonight a problem?"

She laughed. "No, not at all. But not at my shop, please. I'd like the chance to come home, wash the dust off my hands, and change."

"Would six o'clock give you enough time to do all that?" he asked.

"Make it six-thirty," she said. To shower, do her hair and makeup the way she'd want, it would take a little longer. And she wanted to look good for him.

"Oh," he said. "Wear jeans."

Her brow dipped. "Jeans?" She'd had a pretty skirt in mind.

"I'll be picking you up on my bike. Jeans won't get caught in the wheels and they will provide a little protection from the elements. He cocked an eyebrow. "Have a problem with that?"

"No. No. It sounds…" she paused, "exhilarating."

"Now that it's settled, I'll wash, you dry," he said.

"You cooked," she said. "It's only fair that I do dishes."

"I'm used to cleaning up after myself. Besides, it will be more fun if we do it together."

She laughed. "Yes, it will."

He cooked, he did dishes, and he insisted on foreplay. "You're every woman's dream man."

He straightened his shoulders. "I like to think so."

They spent the next few minutes washing and drying the dishes. A few kisses and snuggles were thrown in between passing a plate or a cup.

When they were finished, they spent another thirty minutes in bed making love before she finally had to get up and get ready to go to the shop.

Dressed and ready, they left the house, locking the door behind them.

Duff pulled out of the driveway in Zip's Corvette and waited for Ivy to back out of the garage.

Ivy drove toward her shop in Copperas Cove. When she glanced into her rearview mirror, she noted that Duff followed. When she arrived at her shop's parking lot, she got out and turned to him.

She gave him a crooked smile. "You didn't have to follow me."

"I'd like to check out your shop," he said.

Ivy opened and unlocked the door.

Duff grabbed her arm. "Let me go first."

"You're taking my mother seriously, aren't you?" Ivy frowned.

"Doesn't hurt to be safe," he said.

Ivy unlocked the door and pushed it open. She waved her hand. "Have at it." She liked that he was concerned, but she worried that he was taking her mother's words too seriously.

She watched as he wound his way through her little shop. His big body resembled the bull in the proverbial china shop. Ivy was sure he would knock something over and break it. She didn't care.

She liked watching him.

It didn't take him long to go through the small shop into the backroom office area. Then he returned. "All clear."

She patted his cheek and leaned in to kiss him. "My mother can be a little dramatic. I don't think that it's as serious as she thinks it is."

"Better safe than sorry." He leaned close and crushed his mouth to hers in a kiss that left her toes tingling and her heart hammering. When she opened to him, his tongue found hers and caressed it in a long sexy glide.

She was tempted to tell him that she could open an hour late. It was a really large desk in her office.

"Want me to stay?" he asked.

Oh, the temptation is strong. But she didn't want to make him think that she was needy. "As much as I would like that, I need to get the store ready to open at noon."

He nodded and stepped back. "Six-thirty, then."

She stood at the door and watched as he drove away in the Corvette. Then she locked the door and leaned her back against it.

"Wow." *What just happened?*

She'd just had the best sex of her life.

She pushed away from the door and went to work. Six-thirty couldn't arrive soon enough.

CHAPTER 8

ON HIS WAY back to Killeen, Duff's cellphone chirped. A quick glance at the caller ID indicated Zip was trying to reach him. He answered the phone and hit the speaker button. "Zip."

"Hey, dude," Zip said. "Where are you?"

"You at my house?"

"I am," Zip said. "Though I love your bike, I'm ready to have my 'Vette back."

"I'll be there in five." Duff pressed harder on the accelerator, increasing his speed to five miles an hour over the limit.

When Duff pulled up to his driveway in Killeen, Zip was sitting on his bike with his cellphone to his ear.

Duff got out of the Corvette.

Zip grinned and continued his conversation. "Hey, Des, he's here." He glanced at Duff. "No, I don't see a shit-eating grin, but he does have that after-glow. Yeah...I think he spent the night with Ivy."

Duff glared.

Zip's grin broadened. "Yup. Definitely. He slept with Ivy." He pushed away from the motorcycle and handed Duff the key.

"My sex life has nothing to do with you or anyone else on the team," Duff growled.

"So you admit it?" Zip asked.

Duff had the urge to punch his friend in his smirking mouth. "I admit nothing. I could have been out for donuts and coffee."

Zip looked around Duff to his Corvette. "You didn't bring me any donuts and coffee?"

"I ate there," Duff said, lying through his teeth.

"Uh-huh." Zip crossed his arms over his chest. "At Ivy's house?"

Duff tossed Zip's keys to him. "I was going to ask if you wanted to go hit the dirt bike track with me, but never mind."

"I was hoping you'd suggest it," Zip said, looking down at his attire. "I dressed for fun, just in case."

Duff opened the garage using the keypad and pushed his street bike into an empty space beside three dirt bikes.

Zip walked to one with a bright new coat of orange paint. "This the one I helped you bring home from that barn auction?"

Duff glanced over his shoulder. "Yep."

"Man, that thing was just a bunch of pieces. How'd you put it all back together?"

"One piece at a time," Duff murmured. He set his street bike on its stand and turned to Zip. "You want to ride it?"

"You sure it's not going to rattle apart?" Zip asked.

"I've already taken it to the track. It held together just fine. But if you want, you can take the red one."

"No. I'd like to try this one. I feel like I have a stake in it."

"Let's load up."

Duff backed his truck out of the garage and around to his backyard where he kept his motorcycle trailer parked. After he hooked up the trailer, he drove around to the garage.

Between him and Zip, they loaded the two bikes, secured them, and hooked up the trailer lights. Duff went inside for his leathers and the boots he used while riding his dirt bike. He grabbed his helmet and an extra leather jacket and helmet for Zip.

When he emerged from the house, he gave Zip a chin lift. "Ready?"

"I am."

Duff tossed him the helmet and jacket and climbed into his truck.

On the drive to the track, Zip kept glancing over at Duff.

"What?" Duff finally asked.

"Nothing. Just enjoying the fact you're not as cranky as usual."

"I'm not cranky," Duff said. He noted that his voice did sound gruff, even when he wasn't in a bad mood.

"Ivy must be good for you. I'm glad you two met." He chuckled. "And to think, if she hadn't been mugged, you might not have spent the night with her." His smile faded. "It's a good thing you were there when you were."

Duff had been thinking the same thing. "You think it was more than a mugging?"

"What do you mean?"

"You think she'd been targeted?" Duff asked.

"Why would she be targeted?" Zip's brow furrowed. "Unless you know something I don't."

Duff told him about the conversation they'd had with Ivy's mother.

Zip's eyes widened. "Ivy's mother is Senator Fremont?"

Duff nodded, his lips twitching at the senator's approval of him as her daughter's lover.

"What could a senator have gotten into that would make her a target?"

"Something about shutting down illegal arms sales over the border." Duff turned the truck and trailer out onto the highway.

"You think some of the manufacturers are supplying the drug dealers with arms?"

Duff snorted. "It wouldn't be the first time."

"And the good senator is putting a stop to it." Zip shook his head. "I could see how that would make them mad enough to want to hurt her."

Duff's jaw hardened. "And what better way than to hurt her only daughter?" He was beginning to think he should turn around and head back to Copperas Cove and Ivy's little knickknack shop.

"Think she needs a bodyguard?" Zip asked.

"Not sure. She didn't want me hanging around all day. Said she had a gun, but she didn't say where."

Zip glanced his way, his head tilted. "You're worried about her, aren't you?"

"That guy nearly got away with her last night." Duff slammed his palm against the steering wheel. "Damn right, I'm worried about her."

"You really like her, don't you?" Zip chuckled. "The bigger they are, the harder they fall."

"Shut the fuck up," Duff muttered.

"We can go back to Copperas Cove and hang out in her parking lot all day," Zip suggested.

Duff shook his head. "She wouldn't appreciate me scaring away her customers."

Zip nodded. "Good point."

"Besides, I'll see her tonight."

"You have a second date?" Zip whooped.

Duff frowned. "First date. Wouldn't call last night a real date."

"But you spent a night in the Palace of Pleasure with her," Zip argued. "That counts."

"I didn't say I slept with her," Duff growled. "And don't you go giving Ivy a hard time about it."

"Why would I? You're much more fun to rib. It's like poking a bear." Zip started to poke his finger at Duff.

Duff glared hard at him until he dropped his hand.

"Yup," Zip said, turning his smile toward the road ahead. "Like poking a bear. A bear who got laid last night."

If Duff hadn't been driving, he'd have punched Zip. But by then, they had pulled off the highway and down a back road. A few minutes later, they were at the track, unloading the dirt bikes.

Duff took off on the red bike. It was his favorite. It was lean and fast. He felt his best the faster he could go and the more dirt he could sling up in his face.

He raced around the track, jumping the dirt mounts, launching himself and his bike high into the air.

Zip followed at a much slower pace, unused to the speed and intensity of the dirt bike track.

They ran the track several times, even engaging in a little personal competition with some other riders who joined them. Duff had only one mode. Fast. Anything less was unacceptable.

On one jump and curve in the dirt track, he landed hard and almost lost control of his bike. He put down his foot, let his boot skim the dirt, and straightened the handlebars. As soon as he had it under control, he gave the bike all the fuel and flew over the next bump, rising fifteen feet before he slammed hard onto the track.

The more he thought about Ivy and her attacker, the harder he pushed himself. He didn't want to worry about her—or anyone, for that matter. For the past eight years, he'd only been responsible for himself and his team. He had no wife or children to worry about while he was deployed. And he liked it that way.

He also didn't have a wife and children to welcome him home when he got back from deployment. While some of his teammates were greeted at the airport, he walked on through and went home to his empty house and his motorcycles.

As soon as he could, he'd head to the track and ride his frustrations out, going as fast as was humanly possible.

Some would say he was running away from his past. Duff didn't care what anyone said. By moving, he didn't have time to regret his life, grieve for his wife, or the lack of a family. He gained a lot of satisfaction out of restoring things with his hands.

He didn't need anything else or anyone else. He

certainly didn't need to start something with Ivy he had no intention of finishing.

By the time he'd snorted enough dust up his nose, it was well past five in the afternoon.

If he was smart, he'd cancel his date with Ivy, go home, pop open a bottle of beer, and find a game on the television. Going out with the woman only made it more difficult to break it off with her. And he knew he had to break it off before either one of them felt the need to be together.

Zip stopped his dirt bike next to the trailer ramp where Duff stood with his machine. He dismounted and pulled off his helmet. "Dude, how do you do it?"

Duff set his helmet on the motorcycle seat. "Do what?"

"Go so fast? How do you do it and not kill yourself?" Zip asked, shoving a hand through his hair.

"Takes practice," Duff said. "I've been doing this for years."

"I take it this is what you do instead of dating." Zip shook his head. "Maybe I'm wasting my time dating all those women. Now that I have Destiny, I don't have to date multiple women. I'll have more time. Maybe I can start riding motorcycles."

Duff chuckled. "Most women don't like it when their men ride. Too dangerous."

"I'm sure Destiny wouldn't mind," Zip said.

Duff cocked an eyebrow. "It might end up a

choice between your lady and bike riding. You need to ask yourself which you'd rather give up."

"Neither," Zip said.

"Seriously, though. Which would you give up?" Duff asked.

"The motorcycles," Zip said. "I wasted too many years thinking Destiny didn't want to be near me after my brother died, and then I worked too hard convincing her to take me back after I fucked up. Without a doubt, she's the one for me."

"How'd you know she's the one?" Duff asked.

"Knew it since we were kids, man. She's brave, smart and she gets me."

Zip loaded the motorcycle Duff loaned him on the trailer. Duff pushed his up behind Zip's. They secured the bikes.

"What about you?" Zip asked.

Duff's eyes narrowed. "What do you mean what about me?"

"Do you think Ivy could be the one for you?" Zip asked.

"We haven't been out on our first date." He raised his hand. "Real date."

"Even if I was too young to realize it," Zip said, "deep down, I knew the first time I met Destiny that she was the one for me."

Duff frowned. Deep down, he couldn't deny having the same thoughts about Ivy. That's what had scared him so much. With those thoughts had come guilt.

Katie had been his high school sweetheart practically from his first day of freshman year. She'd been there through his graduation and waited for him when he'd gone off for Army training.

When he'd come back, they'd gotten married.

It had always been Katie. He hadn't imagined himself with anybody else. From the time they'd met to the time Katie had died, they'd known each other for eight years.

Another eight years had passed since Katie died. Was eight years of grieving enough for someone who'd been with him as long?

Zip tossed his helmet into the truck's back seat and climbed into the front passenger seat.

Duff laid his helmet in the back seat and slid in behind the steering wheel.

"So, what's the story?" Zip asked. "You haven't dated a woman for more than a one-night stand since I can remember."

Duff's team didn't know his background. Katie had died before Duff had joined Delta Force. He'd seen no need to inform them about that part of his life. He didn't need their sympathy. What was done was done. Katie was gone.

"No story," Duff said.

"Oh, come on," Zip said. "You must have had

someone in your past who did you wrong and turned you against women."

"I have nothing against women," Duff said. A long pause stretched between them as the miles raced past.

Zip frowned across the console. "You're not going to stick me with the silent treatment, are you?"

Duff nodded. "It's worked for me so far."

"Fine," Zip said. "Wanna swing by that little shop in Copperas Cove where Ivy works? It's on the way home."

Duff's lips twisted. "It's not even close to on the way home. No." Although, he'd had the same thought. He'd like to swing by Ivy's shop and make sure she was okay.

Copperas Cove was a good twenty miles away to get there and back. Duff didn't want to appear overzealous or like a stalker.

Ivy had made it clear that she was an independent woman who could take care of herself. She might resent his interference or declare him creepy for checking up on her at the store.

"Have it your way," Zip said. "I'm sure I could do a little shopping while there. Destiny likes jewelry and trinkets."

"We're not going," Duff said. "I'm picking her up at six-thirty at her house in Copperas Cove after I've had a shower and washed all the dust off me."

"You should wear something a little fancier. Not jeans and a T-shirt," Zip suggested.

"I'm wearing jeans and a T-shirt tonight," Duff said.

"Does Ivy even like motorcycles?" Zip asked.

Duff hadn't thought about that. "She seemed okay with it when I told her I'd pick her up on my motorcycle."

"Where are you taking her?" Zip asked.

"Out to Belton Lake," Duff said. He'd only just thought of where he'd take her. He hoped she'd like it up there.

"Where all the local teens go to neck?" Zip said with a grin.

"We're not going to neck," Duff said.

"Then why go to the lake?" Zip asked, his brows raised.

"I'm taking her on a picnic." Zip's question reminded Duff he needed to pick up food.

"Did you ask her if she liked picnics?" Zip asked.

"No. Should I have?" Duff's brow dipped.

"Not all women like picnics, or ants in their food," Zip said.

Great. Duff was picking up Ivy in an hour and a half with a plan to take her on a picnic she might not even want to go on.

Well, he'd go prepared to ask her if she wanted to go on a picnic. If she said no, he'd have an alternative dinner in mind. There were plenty of barbeque restaurants that would serve them in their jeans.

In fact, there was a barbeque place with a dance-hall in Lampasas. Maybe he'd take her there.

Zip brought up a good point.

Duff really didn't know all that much about Ivy, other than the fact she was Senator Freeman's daughter, that her life might be in danger and that she made sweet love into the night.

Duff realized that if he hadn't gone biking, the day would have stretched even longer than it had already.

Back at Duff's place, Zip helped him unload the dirt bikes and park them in the garage. They were both covered in a fine layer of dust.

Zip held out his hand.

Duff took it and they shook.

"Good luck on the date tonight," Zip said.

Duff nodded. "Thanks."

"You might want to call Gwen and ask a few questions about Ivy," Zip suggested. "You know, things like what she likes to eat, if she's into motorcycles. You know, important things if you want to make a good first impression."

Zip's cellphone chirped with an incoming text. He glanced down at the screen and grinned. "Ah, there's my girl. That's my cue. I'm out of here. Thanks for the ride today. Let's do it again." He ducked into his

Corvette, read his text, and responded before he shifted into gear and headed for the highway.

Duff chewed on Zip's words as he closed the garage door and went inside. He could call Gwen and find out what kind of food Ivy preferred and if she had any food allergies.

Ivy had appeared to like whatever he cooked. She'd eaten everything he'd made. Then again, he'd only made quesadillas and scrambled eggs.

Hell, he didn't even have Gwen's phone number. To get it, he'd have to call Merlin.

"Yo, Duff," Merlin answered.

"Hey, can I get Gwen's number?" Duff asked.

"As long as you're not hitting on my girl," Merlin responded.

"No, I'm not. I had some questions about Ivy."

Merlin chuckled. "Getting serious, are we?"

Duff already regretted calling his friend and teammate.

"I'll share her number in text," Merlin relented. "I hear you're going out with Ivy tonight."

Duff cringed. News traveled fast within his team. "I am."

"It's good to know a little about your date before you go out together," Merlin noted.

"That's the idea," Duff said.

"Sending," Merlin said. "Good luck on your date tonight."

Why did his team seem to think he had to have good luck on his date? It was just a date.

Having asked Merlin for Gwen's number, Duff couldn't forget about it. Gwen would expect a call.

He dialed her number before he could change his mind.

"Gwen, this is Duff."

"Hi, Duff," Gwen said. "Merlin said you had some questions about Ivy. What do you want to know?"

"I just hung up with him."

She laughed. "He texted me, letting me know you would be calling about Ivy. I take it last night's fiasco didn't end up too bad?"

"You've spoken with Ivy?"

"Not actually. She's not answering my calls."

Duff tensed.

"She did text me that she's been busy at the shop," Gwen added.

He relaxed.

"I have to admit, I've been dying to get all the details. I understand you stayed at her house last night."

"I did."

"Her attacker didn't show up again, did he?" Gwen asked. "That scared me to know someone would attack a woman here in Killeen. You think of things like that happening only in the big cities."

"It can happen anywhere," Duff said.

"I know that, but you don't hear of it that often

around here," Gwen said. "I'm glad you were there to rescue her. I had nightmares last night about the whole thing. But, back to Ivy... What is it you'd like to know?"

"Does she like picnics? Riding on motorcycles? What does she like to eat? Wine or beer? Her favorite color? Food allergies? Basically, the works."

Gwen chuckled. "Whoa. Slow down. That's the most I've ever heard you say. You planning on taking her on a picnic?"

"I was. But if she doesn't like eating outside, I can take her someplace else."

"Picnics are fine. We went on one last month. Brought sandwiches and laid out in the sun, reading. As for riding on motorcycles, if her mother would disapprove, she's all for it."

Duff could understand that. And her mother would probably disapprove. Riding the motorcycle was a go.

"No food allergies. She's not vegan or a vegetarian. She likes chicken. Red meat no more than once a week, and then it's a steak or a big, juicy hamburger. Since you're going on a picnic, I'd take wine, not beer. She likes beer, but only when it's icy cold. A good, dry red wine like a cabernet sauvignon would be good to take along. It's best served room temperature. Her favorite color is aqua, and she can't abide people who lie to her."

"Dogs or cats?" he asked.

"Definitely dogs," Gwen said. "She likes cats, but she's mildly allergic to them. Anything else?"

Duff scratched his dirty head. "Can't think of anything right now."

"The rest you can ask Ivy for yourself." Gwen paused. "She's special and she's trying to make a life outside of her mother's and father's political careers."

Duff doubted Ivy would ever be completely free of her mother's political life. And if Senator Fremont had someone threatening her, it could bleed over onto her only daughter.

Duff had the urge to drive over to Copperas Cove despite Ivy's insistence she would be all right.

If the senator was worried enough to hire even more qualified bodyguards to protect her, she had a serious problem.

Duff resisted the urge to go to Ivy's shop. He hoped she'd call or text him to let him know she was all right. In the meantime, he had until a little after six to get ready for his date. He had to get cracking. His heartbeat picked up at the thought. For the first time in a lot of years, he looked forward to seeing a woman for a second time. He refused to let his time with Ivy be a one-night stand. She'd awakened him from what felt like a very long sleep.

CHAPTER 9

THANKFULLY, the store was busy all day long. Copperas Cove had an annual event going on and people from all over the state had come to enjoy its offerings.

Ivy's store benefited from the influx and it kept her moving throughout the day, answering questions, showing merchandise, and ringing up sales.

She barely had time to think about Duff and their *real* date. Still, she found herself shivering with anticipation over what the evening had in store.

Several times that day, she glanced at her cellphone, wishing Duff would call or text to check in on her. She had to remind herself that she'd told him she was capable of taking care of herself.

As soon as he'd left that morning, she'd gotten her handgun out of her office safe and placed it under the counter beneath the cash register. Not that she expected to have to use it, but more to remind her that she needed to carry it with her and have it at her side at all times.

If her mother was worried enough about threats to herself to hire more experienced professionals to guard her, and then to call her daughter when they hadn't spoken in weeks, the threats had to be real and potentially dangerous.

Halfway through the day, when she caught a five-minute break between customers, Ivy picked up her phone to call Duff. That's when she realized she didn't have his phone number. And she hadn't given him hers.

She started to dial Gwen to have her get Duff's number from Merlin but stopped before the call could go through.

Her hand froze before engaging the call.

No.

She didn't want to appear too eager. She hadn't needed a man in her life.

Up until now. And not because she needed protection.

She didn't *need* anything.

But she *wanted* so much more.

And Duff had given it to her.

He wasn't one of the stiff shirts she'd worked with at the law firm. He hadn't passed the bar and he worked with his hands.

Oh, and those hands...

Her heart beat faster, as she remembered what he did with his hands...and his mouth.

Her core heated and she moaned aloud.

The bell over the door jangled, pulling her back to the present, and a gaggle of women came in laughing and smiling from spending their day exploring the area and shopping.

Ivy would have to wait until six-thirty to see Duff again. She hoped their first real date would be every bit as good as their first night together.

The day zoomed by, but as her closing time approached, Ivy found herself watching the clock and counting down the minutes until she could lock the shop and head home for a shower and a change of clothing.

The dress she'd worn throughout the day had wilted a little in the heat and dust of moving merchandise from the back storage room out to the front to fill empty shelves.

She looked forward to wearing jeans and a pretty blouse. Her mother never let her ride with the boys on the backs of their motorcycles growing up. This would be a new experience for her. She wanted to feel the wind in her face. More than that, she wanted to have her arms and legs wrapped around Duff.

A minute before five o'clock, a group of women entered.

"Are you still open?" one of them called out.

As much as Ivy wanted to tell her she closed in

exactly one minute, she smiled and nodded. "Come on in."

The ladies spent the next thirty minutes perusing the candles, pillows and jewelry Ivy had on display. Finally, they selected items and came to the register to check out.

At five forty-five, Ivy left the shop, climbed into her SUV and hurried home. By the time she walked into her house, dropped her purse on the counter and glanced at the clock, she had only thirty minutes to shower, do her hair and makeup and be ready for Duff to pick her up.

Her heart pounding, she raced through the house, gathering jeans, a pretty pale yellow knit top and sexy underwear.

In the bathroom, she turned on the shower and stepped in before the water warmed. She thought it was just as well that it cooled her libido before Duff arrived, or they might not make it back out of the house to go on that motorcycle ride.

At the thought of staying home, her body heated along with the water.

She shampooed her hair quickly and squirted some conditioner into it, rinsing thoroughly. Using one of her favorite bodywash scents, she scrubbed her skin and let the spray wash the suds down the drain.

Switching the water off, she reached for a towel

and dried off, her body super sensitive in anticipation of seeing Duff again.

Ivy threw on her clothes and ran a brush through her hair. She turned on the hairdryer and flipped her hair upside down to dry the underside.

A glance at the clock made her squeak. Ten minutes wasn't nearly enough time to dry her hair and apply makeup.

Turning off the dryer, she worked the makeup, finishing as the doorbell rang. A quick brush through her damp hair and she ran for the door.

She stood for a moment, willing her pulse to slow and the heat in her cheeks to abate, counting to ten before she opened the door.

One, two, three...

Unable to wait a moment longer, Ivy yanked open the door. Her chest swelled and the heat in her cheeks sank low in her belly, making her channel slicken with moisture.

Magnus McCormick stood before her in freshly pressed jeans, a white button-down, long-sleeve shirt, and a bolo tie. His dark hair was neatly slicked back and he held out a small bouquet of slightly crushed flowers.

"Sorry, they got a little ruffled on the ride over," he said.

She took the flowers and sniffed their fragrance. "They're beautiful," she said, her normally clear, concise tone nothing more than a breathy whisper. Why did this man steal her breath away?

"You're beautiful," he said, staring at her face, his gaze then slowly traveling down the length of her body to her bare feet.

He opened his arms.

She stepped into them and he held her, crushing the flowers between them. "I've looked forward to this all day long," he murmured against her damp hair.

"Me too." When she lifted her face to his, he claimed her lips in a soul-defining kiss that left her knees weak and her heart beating erratically against her ribs.

"Ready?" he asked.

Ivy nodded. "So ready," she whispered.

Duff chuckled. "You might want to wear some shoes. Boots would be even better. And if you have a leather jacket, that would be good."

"In this heat?" she asked, leaning back to look up into his face.

"In any weather." He kissed her forehead. "If we have a wreck, you have a better chance of keeping your skin with a leather jacket on."

"Oh." Ivy frowned. "What are the chances of having a wreck?"

"With me? Slim to none." He winked. "It's the other people on the road we have to worry about."

"Got it." She stepped out of his arms, already wanting to be back in them. "I'll be right back."

"Hurry. Our dinner is sitting in the sun."

She ran for her bedroom, grabbed socks, her leather boots and a brown leather jacket. She plunked them on the counter in the bathroom and made quick work of braiding her damp hair into one thick plait at the back of her neck.

When she was finished, she shoved her feet into the socks and boots and grabbed her jacket.

When she came back out, she smiled. "Ready."

"Keys?" he asked.

Ivy grabbed them out of her purse. "Do I need to take my purse?"

"Not unless you're going to use it to buy fish food at Belton Lake."

Her brow dipped. "We're going to the lake?"

He nodded. "I thought a picnic would be nice and, if we're lucky, we might catch the meteor shower that's supposed to be happening tonight."

Ivy quivered in anticipation. It didn't get dark until later that evening. Which meant he had plans to be with her for more than a few hours.

"That sounds lovely."

He nodded. "Good. Otherwise, I was going to take you to Lampasas to a barbeque place I know out there and a dancehall afterward."

"That sounds nice, too." She smiled. "But I think

the lake sounds more relaxing, and I've had a very busy day at the store."

His brow dipped. "Any trouble?"

"None at all. Just a bunch of customers keeping me hopping."

"Right. You're there alone." He frowned.

She was impressed he'd remembered that from her conversation with her mother. "I just opened a month ago, and I'm waiting to see if the place generates enough money to hire help."

"Sounds like a lot of work."

She shrugged into her jacket. "I love it."

"Better than lawyering?"

She nodded. "Much. That was always my mother's dream. Not mine. I was too obedient to tell her different."

"And now?" Duff asked.

"Now, I realize I need to follow my own dreams."

"Will you ever go back to law?"

She lifted her shoulders and let them fall. "Maybe. If I do, it will be to advocate for people who can't afford to hire the high-powered, expensive law firms. People who really need help to make things right in their worlds."

"Very altruistic." He held the door for her. "You sacrificed a lot to make it through law school. Seems a shame not to cash in on your knowledge."

As she stepped across the threshold, she smiled up at him. "You sacrificed a lot to become Delta Force.

Seems you could get paid a lot more by going into the private security business." She cocked an eyebrow in challenge.

"I do it because I love it and believe in the results," he said.

She nodded. "If I go back to law, I'll do it because I want to help others and believe in the results."

"Fair enough." He took her keys from her and locked her front door. Then he handed back the keys and took her hand. "Are you good with riding on the back of my motorcycle?"

She nodded. "I am."

"If not, I can go back and get my truck," he offered.

Ivy shook her head. "I'm looking forward to the wind in my face to clear a few cobwebs."

He brushed a loose strand of her hair back behind her ear. "I don't see any cobwebs," he said and kissed the tip of her nose.

"No?" She leaned up on her toes and pressed her lips to his. "I thought I saw a few on your face yesterday. Seems they've disappeared today."

"Put it down to a night with you," he brushed his lips across hers, "and an afternoon on the dirt bike track."

Ivy laughed. "I think the afternoon on the dirt bike track would have more of an impact."

"It would have, if I'd crashed."

That made her laugh.

He handed her a helmet. "But the night with you wins, hands down."

Her chest swelled at the resonance in his tone. His words and his expression made her feel beautiful, with and without her clothes on. At that moment, she had the overwhelming urge to grab his hand and drag him into her house for the clothes-off version.

He slipped the helmet over her head and buckled it beneath her chin.

She'd look kind of funny wearing a helmet back into the house, so she waited while he put his on and buckled.

Then he mounted the big motorcycle and scooted forward to give her room to sit behind him.

Ivy swung her leg over the bike and sat behind him, wrapping her arms around his waist and her legs around his hips and thighs.

She'd thought about this position all day long. She couldn't imagine it could get any better, until he got the motor humming. The rumble of the engine, the man between her thighs and her arms around his waist made her hotter than the leather jacket and ready for anything. As long as it was with this man.

He drove out of her driveway, her neighborhood and Copperas Cove, heading east.

Most of the rush-hour traffic from Ft. Hood had dissipated, leaving the usual traffic to navigate through.

Thirty minutes later, Duff left the highway and

drove a curving road to get to Belton Lake.

Ivy leaned into him, loving the scent of leather and male. At one point, he laid a hand over hers, in a reassuring way before placing it back on the handle.

Ivy slid her fingers beneath his jacket to the crisp, white shirt, loving the feel of his tight muscles beneath.

All too soon, they arrived at a bluff overlooking the lake. An open, grassy area stretched out in front of them with a few trees close to the edge, providing shade.

Duff drove off the road and parked the motorcycle beneath the shade of one of the trees.

Ivy climbed off the back, shed her helmet and helped him unload the storage compartments on either side.

He pulled out a Mexican blanket in bright shades of orange, blue and red. He laid it out on the ground and anchored it from the wind with a bottle of wine on one corner and an insulated container on the other.

Ivy was glad they hadn't gone to one of the more populated day-use areas. She liked having Duff all to herself.

Duff dropped down on the blanket and opened the insulated container, pulling out cartons of food, including fried chicken, potato salad, dill pickles and fresh peaches.

Another container held paper plates, plastic stemless wine glasses and a corkscrew.

While Ivy dished up the food, Duff opened the bottle of wine and poured two glasses.

Ivy handed him a plate full of chicken and sides. Duff handed her a glass of wine.

They touched the rims of their wine goblets together.

"To getting to know each other," Duff said.

"Hear, hear," she said and drank a long swallow.

"So, your favorite color is aqua?" he said.

Her brow twisted. "How did you know?"

He looked to the sky. "A birdy told me."

"Gwen?" she asked, liking that he'd gone to the trouble of finding out more about her.

He sipped his wine before saying, "Would you think I was stalker if I said yes?"

"Yes."

"Would you care?"

She sighed and picked up a fork. "Did she tell you that I liked fried chicken, too?"

He nodded. "She might have mentioned that you liked chicken more than red meat."

"Good call," she said, picking up a juicy chicken leg. "Although a good steak is always well received."

"She said that, too." He bit into a piece of the chicken and chewed before swallowing. "And she told me not to break your heart."

"Don't worry. I can—"

"—take care of yourself," he finished for her. "I

learned that one from you."

"You know more about me than I do about you," Ivy said with a frown. "My turn."

He raised his hands, palms up. "Go."

"Your favorite color?" she asked.

"Green."

"Why green?" she shot back.

"It's the color of grass and the leaves on the trees in the spring and summer. It's also the color of your eyes." He closed his. "What color are my eyes?"

"No fair," she said. "We're only just getting to know each other."

"That's what I said to Gwen when I called her." His eyes still closed, he asked again, "What color?"

Ivy closed her own and thought back to all the times she'd stared into his and fallen deeper. "Brown."

He opened his eyes and nodded. "Good guess."

She snorted. "I knew. You just surprised me and put me on the spot."

"Best rock band of all time?" he asked.

"That's easy. The Beatles. They laid the framework for the rest."

He nodded. "Best sports team?"

"Aggies," she replied. "My undergraduate alma mater. I attended every home game."

He shook his head. "Longhorns."

"We'll have to agree to disagree."

"True." He ate a bite of the potato salad.

"Beach or mountain vacation?" she asked.

"Mountains in the summer," he said. "Beach in the fall after the kids go back to school. I like a long walk on the sand at sunset. And I like the cool of the higher elevations in the heat of the summer."

Ivy smiled. "Me, too."

"Fish?" he asked.

"Eat or catch?"

"Both," he said.

She nodded. "That's one thing my father taught me at a young age. He wanted a son. Thankfully, I enjoyed fishing, and I didn't babble out on the boat. Lakes, deep sea and ice fishing. I love them all."

"Ice fishing?"

"My father took me on a fishing vacation in Minnesota one year and we fished on the ice in a little hut."

"Your mother?"

Ivy smiled. "Wouldn't be caught dead with a fishing pole in her hands. It was the only time I had my father all to myself."

"You had a good relationship with your father?"

She nodded. "I did. And I had a good one with my mother, though we can be too much alike."

"How so?"

"Both of us are hard-headed and stubborn. I went along with her and my father's idea of what I should do with my life, to a point. When I reached that point, I pushed back and started down my own path."

"Giving up law to own your gift shop?"

She nodded. "My mother was livid. Like her, I didn't back down from what I believed in. Hopefully, she'll get over it eventually. She's all the family I have left."

"Your father was the governor of Texas. How was that?"

"He always made time for me. It might not be much, but he made the effort." Her eyes misted. "He was a good man and a great governor. He led with his heart." Ivy popped a fork full of potato salad into her mouth and chewed.

"And your mother?" Duff asked.

She swallowed. "She also follows her convictions. The lobbyists are frustrated with her. She can't be bought."

"Do you think they're playing dirty with her and sending thugs out to bring her down?" Duff asked.

"Could be," Ivy said. She lifted her wine goblet and took a sip. "What about you? Family?"

"Parents moved to Florida when Dad retired. Mom thought it was hot in Texas, but she's finding it's even hotter in Florida. I expect they'll move back eventually."

"Siblings?" Ivy prompted, taking a pickle from the container and biting off a piece. The dill was just sour enough to make her lips pucker.

"Two brothers. One joined the Marines. The other is also in the Army."

Ivy tilted her head. "Is he Delta Force, like you?"

Duff shook his head. "No. He's a Ranger, though, and damn good at what he does."

"He has no desire to join the Delta Force?"

"He has a wife and baby girl. I think he likes being home more often to be with his family. The occasional deployment is manageable. Delta Force is always on call and ready to deploy at a moment's notice."

"And you like that?" Ivy asked.

He shrugged. "Never had a reason to dislike it."

"You almost did," she said quietly.

"Almost is only good in horseshoes and hand grenades," he said.

Ivy held up her hand. "I'm sorry. I didn't mean to bring up a painful subject."

"It's okay. It was a long time ago. Before I joined Delta Force."

She nodded. "Is that the reason you joined?"

He stared out at the water. "Yes. The more intense the training, the less time I had to think."

"And now?"

"Now, I love what I do. I feel like I make a difference."

"Do you still think of her?" Ivy spoke softly.

He nodded. "I do. No matter how many years have gone by, I still ask myself if I could have done more to save her."

"You can't undo the past."

He shook his head. "No." He pushed the cork back into the wine and stood. "Feel like a little exercise?"

She shrugged. "Sure. What did you have in mind? I have to tell you, my pushups aren't up to Army standards. The best I can do is plank for thirty seconds."

He chuckled. "I wasn't thinking of that kind of exercise. How about a hike down to the water and back? My teammates like to take the fast track down by jumping off the rocks into the water, but we're not dressed to swim."

"A hike would be nice. Although, jumping could be fun too. Just not in jeans and boots."

"Next time, we'll wear suits beneath our clothes. The water's deep and cool here."

"You're on." Her heart warmed. He was already talking about a next time. She'd like that. A lot.

Ivy helped pack up the food and wine and put them in the storage compartment on the motorcycle.

Once they'd stored everything, Duff took her hand and helped her find her footing down a narrow trail leading down the side of the bluff to the water below.

He was patient and careful to make sure she didn't fall. Ivy was more worried he'd fall off the trail no wider than a goat might travel. He was a big guy. Yet, he descended the path with a sureness of foot that Ivy envied.

A small area of rocks and sand waited at the

bottom. They stripped off their boots and waded into the cool lake water. Afterward, they sat on the sand until their feet dried, skipping stones across the smooth surface.

The sun was well on its way to the horizon when they started up the trail to the top of the bluff.

Dusk had settled over the land, blurring the trees with shadows.

"Thank you for a wonderful evening," Ivy said as they neared where they'd parked the motorcycle.

"It's not over yet," he said. "The stars will make their appearance soon, and that meteor shower should start soon after."

"That's right." She hurried toward the motorcycle. "We'll need the blanket."

"And the wine," Duff added, coming up behind her.

A dark shape exploded from the shadows, rushing toward Ivy. Another came at Duff, bent low like a defensive player on a football team.

Ivy screamed and tried to duck to the right to avoid the man rushing toward her.

A third man emerged from behind the tree and hurtled toward Duff.

The two men hit him with their shoulders, square in the gut, grabbed his arms and pushed him to the edge of the bluff.

Ivy dodged her attacker and ran toward Duff.

He fought them, getting a few good punches in

before they lifted him off his feet and sent him flying over the edge of the cliff.

Ivy screamed. A hand clamped over her mouth and around her arms.

She struggled and kicked but couldn't break the hold. Soon, the other two men returned to help her captor carry her back to the road where they'd parked a maintenance van behind a stand of bushes.

"Let me go," she yelled as they shoved her through the side door and onto the metal floor of the van.

She landed on her hands and knees and scrambled backward, trying to get out.

Two men climbed in after her. One yanked her arms behind her and sat on her legs while the other secured her wrists together with duct tape. They taped her ankles together next.

"Get the hell off me. You can't do this!" She screamed again, the sound filling the van, deafening her ears.

The guy who'd bound her wrists and legs slapped a piece of tape over her mouth and muttered a curse at her in Spanish.

Once they'd secured her hands and feet, the two men left her in the middle of the van floor. One climbed into the passenger seat beside the driver. The other sat against the door working with a black case.

Ivy rolled and squirmed, desperate to get out of the van and back to Duff.

Sweet Jesus, she hoped he'd hit the water, not the rocks below. She had to get away and go for help.

Her captor by the door withdrew a syringe from the case, stuck it into a small vial and withdrew liquid. Then he set the case and the vial aside and came toward her.

Ivy froze. She couldn't let him stick that needle into her. Duff's life could depend on her ability to get away. She didn't give a damn about herself, but Duff didn't deserve to die because of her. He *couldn't* die. He was a good guy, someone she could see herself with for the long-term.

She'd just found him. It couldn't end like this.

As the man approached her, Ivy lay perfectly still. When he was close enough, she turned on her side and shoved her legs at him, hitting him full in the gut.

He flew backward, hitting the door with a hard thud. Muttering curses, he came at her again, this time from behind, avoiding her legs this time. When he got close enough, he sat on her knees.

Ivy couldn't move. She tried, but she couldn't even roll out of position.

The man jabbed the needle into her arm and emptied it into her.

Her vision blurred and her head spun. She closed her eyes and prayed Duff was all right.

Please. Please be all right.

Darkness consumed her.

CHAPTER 10

DUFF HIT THE WATER HARD. Air shot from his lungs on impact, before he sank beneath the surface.

As he dropped toward the bottom, he thought, *How just.* How fitting that his death hadn't been from being shot at or blown up by an IED or mortar round. That he should die by drowning seemed appropriate after he'd allowed Katie the same sentence.

Stunned by the jolt when he hit, he drifted slowly, unable to move, unable to do anything but let the water take him down to the murky depths of the lake.

As he sank, he looked up at the light, wondering if his body would be found in a day, a month, a year. Not really caring that he would die.

When he touched the bottom, something clicked inside.

Those men who'd shoved him over the cliff hadn't wanted to kill him so much as get him out of the way.

So they could take Ivy.

Motion returned to his body. He bunched his legs beneath him and kicked off the giant boulders at the bottom of the lake, shooting himself upward toward the surface.

Ivy was in trouble. She needed him, and he was at the bottom of the lake, useless to help her.

They could be a county away by now, and he would never catch up. He couldn't let them hurt her. He'd just found her. Found the one for him.

Like Zip said, as soon as he'd met her, he'd known. At least he'd known in his subconscious. His stupid consciousness had stood in his way of admitting it. Guilt over loving another woman who wasn't Katie had held him back.

But Ivy. She was amazing. Smart, beautiful, independent, and determined. What more could he want in a life partner?

If he didn't get out of the lake and find her, he might not get that chance to ask her to be with him for the rest of their lives, no matter how long that might be.

She made him want more out of life. She made him want to take another chance on love.

When he thought his lungs might burst or that he'd have to inhale and suck in a shit load of water, he burst through the surface and out into the open air.

Sucking in lungs full of air, he swam to shore and ran up the narrow game trail to the top.

His bike was there, but Ivy wasn't.

Thankfully, the men who'd taken her hadn't touched his motorcycle. His cellphone was toast, having gone over the cliff and into the lake in his pocket. He shook it and prayed for reception or that it would even turn on. Alas, it didn't.

Duff leaped onto his motorcycle and raced down the road and out onto the highway, speeding up to eighty miles per hour.

When a policeman got behind him with his blue lights flashing, Duff sent up a prayer to the heavens to send help his way.

He pulled over, jumped off his motorcycle, and ran toward the police car.

The officer emerged from his service vehicle, gun drawn. "Stop right there and put your hands up," he called out.

"I'm not the criminal," Duff said, his hands in the air. "My girlfriend and I were attacked. They pushed me into the lake and took my girlfriend. You have to help me."

"I don't have to do anything. Give me your driver's license. Make any sudden moves and I'll shoot."

"Reaching for my wallet," Duff called out. He kept

one hand in the air and reached into his wet back pocket and extracted his sodden billfold. He tossed it to the officer and raised his hand again. "I'm a soldier from Ft. Hood. My girlfriend is Ivy Fremont, Senator Elizabeth Fremont's daughter. Call your supervisor, get him to get Senator Fremont on the phone. She'll know me, and she'll know that I'm telling the truth."

The officer pulled out Duff's license and called in the number to dispatch.

"Please," Duff begged. "The sooner we put out an alert, the better chance we have of finding her. There's no telling where they'll take her."

The officer ignored his entreaties, continuing to talk on his radio to dispatch. Finally, he looked up. "Mr. McCormick, you realize you were going eighty-five miles per hour in a fifty-five zone?"

Anger burned in Duff. "Do you not understand? My girlfriend was kidnapped. The men who took her tried to kill me. You're damn right I was going over the speed limit. My cellphone was waterlogged when they pushed me over the cliff into the lake. I couldn't call 911."

Another police car arrived, lights flashing.

An older man got out. He spoke to the original officer and then turned to Duff. "I got a hold of Senator Fremont's assistant. She was able to confirm that a Magnus McCormick is in fact dating her daughter. The question is, how do we know you weren't the one to kidnap her daughter?"

"Because I was pushed into the lake. I couldn't kidnap her daughter when I was trying not to drown. Could you at least let me borrow your cellphone so that I can call 911 and report a missing person, since you aren't taking me seriously?"

The radio crackled. The older police officer stepped away to answer the call while the younger one continued to point his service weapon at Duff.

"You don't seem to understand," Duff said. "My girlfriend is in danger. Please, let me use a cellphone. I need to call my friends if you're not going to do anything about it."

The older police officer returned. "Let him go. His story pans out. The senator has had threats to herself and her family. The chief put out an APB for the return of Senator Fremont's daughter. Roadblocks are being set up on the interstate and on the roads leading out of Belton and Killeen." The man held out his cellphone. "Sir, you can use my personal cellphone. Sorry for the trouble."

Duff grabbed the phone and dialed Merlin's number. "Merlin, Duff here. Need to gather the team."

"What's up?" Merlin asked. "Why are you calling on this number?"

"They got Ivy."

"When?"

Duff gave a brief version of what happened. "We need to get Senator Fremont on the horn and find out who we're dealing with and where they might have taken her."

"Where are you now?" Merlin asked.

"Near Lake Belton on my way to Killeen."

"Meet me at my place. I'll have the others assemble here. ETA?"

"Ten minutes." Duff ended the call and handed the phone back to the police officer.

"If you'd like a police escort, we've been instructed to provide one."

"I'll take you up on it," Duff said. "As long as we can exceed the speed limit."

"You've got it," the older officer said.

Both police officers jumped into the cars as Duff mounted his motorcycle.

The older officer took the lead, followed by Duff and then the younger officer.

They pushed ninety all the way into Killeen. Once Duff turned off the main road, the police officers disengaged.

Moments later, Duff pulled up to Merlin's place.

His team came out of the house to greet him.

"You all right?" Zip asked.

"Heard you took a fall off a cliff, man." Jangles clapped him on the back. "Glad you made it out of the lake."

Woof poked his head out the door. "Merlin's got the senator on the phone. You need to get in here."

Duff entered Merlin's place. Merlin stood at the

table with his tablet propped up and a video call in progress with Ivy's mother.

"Magnus," she said as he came into view of the tablet's webcam. "I thought you were the man to keep my daughter safe."

"I'm sorry, ma'am. We'll find her."

"I think I can help you."

"How so, ma'am?"

"If she's wearing the necklace I gave her for her last birthday, it has a tracking device embedded in it."

Hope bloomed in Duff's chest. "She was wearing a necklace."

"Was it gold with a green pendant?" the senator asked.

"Green the color of her eyes?" he asked.

"That's it."

"Yes. She was wearing it."

"I've got my men on it. They're pulling it up now. How big a head start did they get?"

"From the time I hit the water to the time I called Merlin, about thirty minutes."

"They could be anywhere in thirty minutes," Zip said.

"Wait. They've got a location," the senator said. She turned away from her webcam. "Where?"

Duff held his breath and waited.

She turned back to Duff. "Apparently, there's a small general aviation airport near Killeen." She turned back to whoever she was talking with. "It's

Skylark Field. The tracker indicates that's where she is."

"I'm on it." Duff spun and was out the door in two seconds.

He heard Merlin call out, "Zip, give him your cellphone."

Zip followed. "Here, take my phone since yours is out of commission. I'll be right behind you." He jumped into his Corvette and followed Duff down the highway.

Duff pulled into the terminal and was off his motorcycle before the engine completely shut down. Zip's phone rang in his pocket. He pulled it out to see Merlin's number. "Yeah," he answered.

"Fremont says the tracking device is out on the tarmac about fifty yards straight out from the terminal.

Inside, he approached the counter. "I need to get out on the tarmac."

"Sir, I'll need to see your ID and know your reason for going out on the field." She held out her hand.

"My girlfriend was kidnapped, and we think she might be out on the field right now."

"I'll still need to see your ID." Her hand still out, she waited.

Zip ran inside. "What's the hold-up?"

Duff threw his wallet at the woman. "My ID is in

there. If she's out there, we have to get to her before they take off with her."

The woman took out his military ID. "You can go." She hit a button behind the counter, opening the sliding glass doors leading out onto the tarmac.

Duff raced through the door.

Behind him, he heard the woman say, "Not you," to Zip. "I'll need to see your ID."

Duff didn't wait. "Fifty yards," he said with the cellphone on speaker.

Merlin responded. "Give or take."

Duff stared out at the tarmac. "Straight out?" He slowed to a halt.

"Straight out from the FBO."

"There's nothing there," he said, his tone flat, his heart sinking to his knees.

"There has to be. The tracker shows her there." Duff walked out fifty yards, searching the ground. Something glinted in the sunshine. He hurried toward the shiny object and bent to find the necklace Ivy had worn that day and the night before. "I found her necklace. She's not here."

Zip ran up behind him. "That's the device?"

Duff nodded and looked to the sky. "She was here." He turned and ran back to the terminal. The door slid open. "What aircraft just took off?"

"Sir, I can't answer that question."

"Do you know what plane just left from here?"

"The plane that was out on the tarmac didn't

require fuel. I don't have a record of his tail number," the woman said. "If they filed a flight plan, you can look them up on one of the flight tracking apps."

"Which one?" Duff asked.

The woman showed him how to download the app on Zip's cellphone.

"What's happening," Merlin's voice came over the cellphone's speaker.

"Hold a minute," Duff said as the app came online.

"There," the receptionist said and pointed to the green dotted line where a plane had left the small airport. "That has to be it. Click on the tail number and it will bring up the flight plan."

He clicked on the tail number and the flight plan came into view.

Duff cursed.

"Costa Rica?" Zip said, leaning over Duff's shoulder.

"They're headed to Costa Rica?" Merlin asked over the speaker.

"Looks that way," Duff said.

"Do we have time to scramble military aircraft to divert them?" Merlin asked.

"No," Duff said. "They're almost to the Mexican border. And what could military aircraft do? Shoot them down?" He shook his head. "We want to save Ivy, not kill her."

"I'll work with her mother to see if we can contact

any special agents on the ground in Costa Rica to intercept the plane when it lands."

"Heading back to your place," Duff said. "Anything they can do will help."

"In the meantime, I'll contact the CO and see what we can do to scramble our team for an extraction."

"To Costa Rica?" Duff asked, a fleeting spark of hope growing inside.

Merlin snorted. "Where else?"

CHAPTER 11

Ivy woke with a splitting headache, her hands and feet numb and pain in her hip where she'd been laying on a hard floor for who knew how long.

She opened her eyes to sunlight finding its way around blinds in a window above her. Not her room. Not her bed. *Where the hell am I?*

Slowly, the events following her picnic at the lake with Duff came back to her and she jerked to full wakefulness.

Duff.

Tears welled in her eyes. Had he survived the fall from the cliff? God, she hoped he had.

If she got out of the restraints holding her wrists and ankles, she'd kick some ass.

Ivy twisted and turned in an attempt to sit and take stock of her surroundings. Nothing about them was familiar. Even the smell.

She heard voices on the other side of a wooden door. They were speaking Spanish. She wished she could remember even half of what she'd learned of Spanish in the two years she'd taken it during her undergraduate degree at Texas A&M University.

She had no idea where they'd taken her or how long she'd been unconscious. All she knew was that she couldn't rely on anyone else. No one knew where she was. She had to get herself out of this situation. Whatever they wanted from her mother, they wouldn't get. Her mother had a policy...she didn't negotiate with terrorists.

Not even for her daughter.

The room was bare except for a rickety bed with a thin, soiled mattress in one corner, bare of sheets, blankets or a pillow.

The room was stifling hot with no air movement and no sign of air conditioning ducts or a window unit. The walls were some sort of stucco with peeling paint and cracks in the finish, showing the ragged bricks beneath.

If she could get close enough to one of the cracks, she might be able to scrape the tape off her wrists.

Scooting across the floor, she made her way to the wall a few short feet away. Then she turned and backed up, but her wrists were too low to reach the crack while she sat on the floor.

Listening for footsteps, she rolled over and up onto her knees and backed up to the wall again. This time, she could reach the crack with her wrists and began rubbing the tape against the bricks.

She worked at the tape for several minutes, unsure how well it was working, but hopeful that if she rubbed at the duct tape long enough, it would eventually wear through.

Voices sounded on the other side of the door.

Her heart hammering against her ribs, she dropped to the floor and lay on her side with her eyes shut. She opened them a slit. Enough to see what was going on at the door.

Metal scraped against metal as a key was inserted into the lock and turned. The doorknob turned and the door swung open.

A dark-haired man with black, bushy brows entered. He wore a white guayabera shirt and a plethora of gold chains around his neck. He said something in Spanish to someone in another room.

The other person responded in Spanish.

The man crossed the floor and nudged her with his foot.

Ivy played dead, pretending she was still unconscious.

Through the slit in her eyes, she could see the man's eyes narrow. He pulled his foot back and kicked her hard in the side.

Ivy grunted and opened her eyes, blinking as if she were just waking up. "What?" she said. "Who are you? What do you want?"

"So, you are not dead," he said. "That is good. It's hard to negotiate with a corpse."

"Negotiate for what?" she said. "I don't have any money."

The man spit on the floor beside her. "We don't want money. We want what we ordered and paid for."

"I don't know what you're talking about," she said, making her voice sound groggier than she felt.

"You don't, but your mother does. We will get what we want, or she'll get her only daughter back in a body bag." He grabbed her by the hair and yanked her up into a sitting position. "The senator has demanded proof of life." The man held a cellphone in front of her. "Say hello *a tu madre*."

Ivy stared at the phone, her lips pressed into a thin line.

"Say hello." The man demanded again.

When she didn't open her mouth or say anything, he kicked her in the side, hard enough she fell over.

Pain shot through her where he'd kicked her and where she'd hit the floor. Still, she refused to say anything.

"Have it your way. Blood always makes these things move faster." He yanked her up again by the hair and punched her in the side of the face.

The temple that had been injured in her last altercation exploded in agony. Warm liquid oozed down her face. She swayed.

If the man hadn't been holding onto her hair, she would have toppled over.

He held the cellphone in her face and hit the record button. "You see, she is alive. But she won't be for long if we do not receive the items we have requested in twenty-four hours. Your daughter has exactly twenty-four hours to live. It is your choice. Or her death sentence." He ended the recording and released her hair. "You will do well to cooperate, if you want to live."

He left the room, slamming the door behind him. The scrape of a key in the lock indicated they weren't taking any chances of their bargaining chip getting away.

Her head still spinning from the blow, Ivy sat for a moment, waiting for her vision to clear.

When it finally did, she rolled onto her knees, leaned against the wall and worked at the tape binding her wrists. When she got free, she'd find a way to get out of the room. And if she had a chance, she'd give that man a bit of what he'd given her.

For over what felt like a lifetime but was probably only a little over an hour, she rubbed away at the tape until slowly, the threads of the material wore through and popped, one by one.

Hope built with every thread broken until she finally broke through the last one binding her wrists. She pulled one hand free and brought her arms back to her front and removed the rest of the tape and a layer of skin with it. Raw and red, her wrists were free. Quickly, she worked at the tape around her ankles until they too were free, and she could stand and work the blood back into her feet.

When she stood, the first place she went to was the window. She opened the shutter and peered out into bright sunlight. It blinded her for a moment. When her eyesight adjusted, she could see that the window had iron bars over the opening. There was no glass, so she reached out and tested the strength of the iron bars. At first, they didn't budge. She pushed hard on the iron, and then pulled, bracing her feet against the wall to add leverage. Again, she pushed, leaning her entire body into the effort. The sound of stucco crumbling gave her the courage to keep going.

What she needed was a pry bar.

Ivy let go of the iron bars and turned back to her room. The single-wide bed was built with wooden legs and she suspected the frame was metal.

She hurried to the bed, dragged the mattress aside, and studied the frame—metal, as she'd suspected. Like the cracked stucco, the bed had seen better days.

If she could just...break the legs free. Ivy tested all the legs. Grasping the loosest post, she twisted it back and forth, wiggling and jostling. The screw holding it to the metal frame loosened. A couple more twists and the leg came off.

She ran back to the window and shoved the leg

between the iron bars and the wall. Pulling the end of the post, she heaved all of her strength and weight into it.

The iron bars shifted suddenly.

The leg slipped from her hands and fell through the bars and onto the ground outside.

Ivy almost cried with her frustration. She pushed at the iron bars. Though they moved, they didn't dislodge from the window.

She hurried back to the bed and eyed the metal frame, wondering how she could dismantle it without a wrench and screwdriver. She couldn't. Instead, she worked at another wooden leg, hoping it would break off as easily.

It didn't. It took her another thirty minutes, bending, pushing, stomping on, and bruising her fingers, arms, and legs in an attempt to break it free. When she was about ready to give up, it cracked at the screw holding it to the frame and came loose.

Holding the treasured bed leg in her hand, Ivy raced back to the window and wedged the leg between the iron bars and the wall again, this time in a different section. She pushed hard, leaning all of her weight onto the wooden leg. The wall outside cracked and shifted.

Ivy held tightly to the leg, refusing to lose another. She almost laughed at the thought of going through all the bed legs until she was on her last leg.

Her internal pun put a smile on her face when it hurt to smile.

The iron bar grate snapped free of the outer wall at the bottom.

Ivy quickly moved the bed leg to the upper portion of the iron bars and shoved it between the bars and the wall. This time, she couldn't leverage her weight; the position was too high.

She dragged the bedframe over to the window. Lucky for her, the legs she pulled off were on opposite corners, so the bedframe still stood flat, though not very secure. Ivy piled the mattress back onto it and stepped up. She gained a good six inches and a better shot at levering the bed leg. She pulled and tugged on the wooden leg but just couldn't get the same amount of leverage she'd gotten below.

Sweating in the heat, she stared at the grate, her hopes diminishing with each passing minute.

I can't give up, damn it.

Ivy threw herself at the iron bars, all the anger at being caught and held captive going into her final push to free herself. The iron bars shoved outward at an angle, held in at the top where she'd been unsuccessful at dislodging it from the wall.

She grabbed the bars, brought them in and shoved them back out, again and again, grunting with the effort.

About to give up, she shoved one last time and leaned all her weight into it.

The bars swung wider this time. Stucco worked free from the wall, showering down on Ivy, and then the whole grate crashed to the ground.

Ivy clapped a hand over her mouth to keep from shouting for joy. She ran to the door and listened for the sound of footsteps running toward her. If the men in the other room had heard the crashing sound, they would come running to check on their captive.

Apparently, the other room didn't have an open window onto the same alley that Ivy had. No one came.

Ivy ran to the window and tried to climb up and over the sill.

The small window made it hard to do. She didn't have enough room to pull herself up to sit on the edge. Ivy tried jumping up and through, using the mattress as a springboard. She got her chest through, but not the rest of her body before she fell back into the room.

The sound of voices coming toward her room made her scramble to close the wooden shutters and move the now-listing bed frame and mattress back into place. She lay down on the floor with her back to the wall, her ankles together, and her hands behind her back, hiding the fact she no longer had tape binding her wrists. Hopefully, they wouldn't notice that her ankles were no longer bound and that two of the bed legs were missing.

The scrape of a key in the lock preceded the big guy in the guayabera shirt's entrance.

His lip curled in a sneer. "*Tu madre* refuses to negotiate. You will appeal to her to change her mind." He grabbed her hair and pulled her to a sitting position and shoved the phone in front of her face.

It was all Ivy could do to keep from slugging the man in his fat, asshole face. She prayed he didn't notice her unbound wrists and ankles. If he looked too closely, he'd see. He might not be as lenient on his second round of beatings.

Ivy played the cowed prisoner and spoke into the video. "Please, Mother, do whatever they say. I can't take much more of this."

The man ended the video and gave her a shove, pushing her over onto her side. She didn't try to save her head from hitting the ground. If she had, she would have given herself away.

Guayabera Man's lip curled. "You Americans think you own us." He snorted. "You own nothing. You're all puppets of your government. A government who wouldn't dare send a rescue team into our country to reclaim one of their own."

Ivy lay still, hiding her hands behind her. She could use a rescue about now. What did it take to call in the Delta Forces to rescue a senator's daughter? Her mother said she didn't negotiate with terrorists. A rescue wasn't a negotiation. Would she pull the right strings to send in the US military to save her daughter?

Ivy loved her mother and, deep down, she prayed her mother loved her enough to send in the cavalry.

Even if she managed to get out of her prison, she still had no idea where she was or how to get back home. She could be in Mexico, South Texas or South America for all she knew.

The odds of finding her way to an American Embassy when she couldn't even speak enough Spanish to find her way to an airport were looking pretty slim.

But staying in her makeshift cell wasn't an option. Not when she had a window to get through.

Guayabera Man left the room, locking the door behind him.

Ivy leaped to her feet, folded the thin, flimsy mattress in two, and climbed on top of it. The added height was just enough to get her head, shoulders, and chest over the sill. To get the rest of the way out she'd have to go headfirst and drop to the ground on top of the metal grate and pray she could navigate her way through whichever country they held her in.

CHAPTER 12

Duff stared around the belly of the C130 aircraft transporting them to Costa Rica through the night and into the early hours of the morning. They had special clearance from the Costa Rican government to land at the *Aeropuerto Internacional de Limón* on the west coast. The same airport where the plane carrying Ivy Fremont had landed earlier that night.

Based on the flight tracking app on Zip's cellphone, the cartel members who'd captured Ivy were a good six hours ahead of them by now.

Fortunately, they'd been able to get DEA agents on the ground in Limón before the plane carrying Ivy landed. They reported that the occupants of the plane were met by a dozen heavily armed men. They unloaded an item that could have been the body of a woman the size of Ivy Fremont.

The agents had followed the SUV they'd loaded

the body into all the way into the jungle. The vehicle entered a village compound known to shelter members of the drug cartel that had connections to the Columbian drug trafficking syndicate running tons of cocaine between Columbia and the US.

The agents were outnumbered and out-gunned. They didn't have the manpower to stage a rescue operation against the cartel.

They were told to stand down and wait for the extraction team.

Not wanting to miss any important events, the DEA agents remained in position outside the jungle village to capture any intelligence about movements that might involve the relocation of the hostage.

They reported via satellite phone every hour, keeping the feds in Washington and the Delta Force team in the loop.

Besides a fourteen-man team of Deltas from Fort Hood, the C130 held three Ultralight Tactical Vehicles and one motorcycle. Sources on the ground in Limón were arranging for two trucks with trailers to meet them on the tarmac.

During the four and half hours it took to fly from Killeen to the airport in Costa Rica, Duff alternated between catnapping and worrying about Ivy. Were they treating her badly? Would they kill her when they realized her mother wouldn't bend to the terrorists' demands? Would the Delta team get to her in time?"

He knew he had to sleep to have the energy to fight whatever battles lay ahead. The rest of his team had leaned back in their web seats, closed their eyes, and at least got the rest they would need when they landed.

Duff's gaze went to the motorcycle. His hands bunched into fists. He wished the plane flew faster. The cartel had given Senator Fremont only twenty-four hours to get the weapons they'd ordered delivered to them. If they didn't get them in the timeframe, they'd kill Ivy.

Duff wasn't going to let that happen. Not on his watch.

He'd thoroughly enjoyed Ivy's company and found her to be the kind of woman he could see himself with for more than a single date.

Yes, they'd only been out on one real date, but he felt like they'd been together for much longer.

He checked his watch for the twentieth time since they'd left the airspace around Ft. Hood and headed south.

They'd be landing in the next ten minutes. He wished he could see the lights of the city below. Sitting in the fuselage with no windows frustrated him. However, he could feel the plane slowing and the landing gear lowering and locking into place.

The team stirred awake, checked their weapons and waited for the aircraft to touch down on the runway.

Finally, the wheels touched the tarmac and the plane taxied to a stop. The ramp lowered and the men filed out, greeted by two liaisons from the US embassy. They held the keys to two trucks equipped with trailers standing to the side of the terminal.

Duff and Merlin, along with Rucker and Lefty, the other two leads from the teams that had been assigned to the mission, were the last men out of the back of the C130. They drove the UTVs and motorcycle out and loaded them onto the trailers. The jungle village was over thirty kilometers from the small airport. The motorcycle would be fine on the road. But they had to get the UTVs closer before they took off on their own and infiltrated the jungle hideout. With the UTVs and motorcycle, they wouldn't have to rely on well-traveled roads to get close enough to make a difference.

Once the lightweight vehicles were loaded and secured on the trailers, they received directions and a word of caution. The jungle would be dangerous. They couldn't see into the dense shadows, but the enemy out there could see and hear them coming if they came down a major road.

Thus the need for the ultralight vehicles. With the smaller, toughened vehicles, they could avoid the main roads and go cross country to the village.

Like they'd practiced on the range at Fort Hood, they created a diversion so that Duff could slip past the guards and into the compound, extract Ivy, and get out before the cartel guards could be alerted.

It sounded easy. But Duff knew better. All good plans were only as good as the start, then all bets were off. He wanted to ride the motorcycle out to the SUV drop-off location, but he needed to conserve the fuel in its tank in case they had to make a run for it from the cartel. They might be on the road for hours before the cartel gave up looking for them and abandoned the village and relocated to another site to manage their drug trafficking operations.

"Load up," Lefty called out.

The men piled into the SUVs. With the GPS coordinates the DEA agents had given, they took off headed away from the city and out along a road toward the southwest, away from the coast and into the rainforest jungle.

As they left the city of Limón, Duff sat forward in the passenger seat of one of the SUVs. Merlin drove. Zip, Woof and Jangles occupied the back seat, leaning toward the windows, peering out at the lush, green landscape.

The sun was rising behind them, turning the sky a bright, light blue.

The road leading into the rainforest seemed to narrow. Trees rose around them, blocking the sunshine and making long dark shadows over the road.

"How long has it been since we've heard from the DEA agents on-site?" Duff asked.

Merlin glanced down at his watch. "Thirty minutes."

"They know we're on our way?" Duff asked.

"Lefty let them know we were coming, giving them an ETA of one hour from the moment we left the airport," Zip said from the back seat. "I heard him talking to them as we left."

Duff gave his friend a nod. "Good."

"As briefed, if we get separated at the compound, make your way out and back to the coast. Don't aim for Limón. That's where they'll look first. Head for the expat community of Cahuita, on the beach south of Limón. Duff has a friend in the community."

"Yeah? Care to share?" Zip grinned. "Male or female?"

Duff frowned. "Male. Vance Tate. He was my neighbor a long time ago when I was stationed at Fort Bragg, North Carolina. He and his wife moved to Costa Rica when he retired."

Vance had been a buyer for a large chain store. Duff and Vance had exchanged numbers. Every once in a while, he'd get a text from Vance, asking how he was doing and where he was stationed.

Duff had always wanted to visit Costa Rica, hearing that the beaches were beautiful, and the interior was fun to explore. He'd wanted to visit the valley with the volcano and surf the western shore.

He wouldn't make it to the western shore on this trip, but he'd get a little taste for the rainforest in their current operation. Not that he cared at that moment. What he was most concerned about was getting Ivy out alive and well.

"The cartel could have spies all over the country and even in government positions. We don't know whether our arrival in Limón was announced before we got there or observed as we landed," Merlin said.

"They could be moving Miss Fremont as we speak," Woof said.

"Our DEA agents would notify us via satellite. And they'd follow, keeping us in the loop," Merlin said.

They stopped five miles short of the cartel's jungle village, pulled the SUVs off the road, and hid them in the underbrush. Moments later, they had the motorcycle and UTVs offloaded and ready, engines warming.

The team gathered around a contour map of Costa Rica spread out on the ground.

"We're to get within a mile of the compound by vehicles and the rest of the way on foot," Lefty said. "Reconnaissance first, reporting guards, locations, and reinforced structures. At nightfall, we move in. If they look like they're moving the hostage, we move in early. We get in, Duff extracts the hostage, and we get out. Rendezvous back here, if possible."

"If shit hits the fan, scatter," Merlin said. "Duff,

you and Miss Fremont will be the most mobile on the motorcycle. You're to make your way to the ex-patriot community of Cahuita. We'll arrange pick up by sea and ferry everyone down to Panama where the C130 will be waiting to return us to the States."

"Even among the expats, be careful," Duff said. "We don't know who's working with the cartel. We can't afford to lose Miss Fremont because we had loose lips."

Merlin nodded. "And if all else fails and Cahuita looks bad, make your way to the US Embassy in San José."

"Comm check?" Rucker called.

One by one, they tested their radio headsets.

Duff checked his weapons and the extra maga-zines of rounds he'd tucked into pockets and slots on his bulletproof vest. His K-bar knife was tucked into the scabbard at his side and his Glock 9mm pistol rested securely in his shoulder holster. He'd also chosen to carry the HK 416 carbine with a short barrel. If he got in a bind, he could shoot his way out. This he had slung over his shoulder with a loose strap. If he needed it, he had it.

Lefty glanced at Rucker and Merlin. "Ready?"

They nodded.

Then as one, every member of the three teams nodded.

"Let's go."

They mounted the UTVs and Duff straddled the motorcycle.

The team paralleled the dirt road as much as possible without actually driving down it. If they had guards out farther than a mile, they'd spot them on the only road leading past the turnoff to the village compound.

As agreed, one mile from the target GPS, they dismounted.

Duff killed the engine but pushed the motorcycle through the woods as he neared the compound, wanting it as close as possible. He'd have to get Ivy out on foot. The sooner they reached the motorcycle, the quicker they could put distance between them and the cartel. The cartel would have the advantage if they discovered Ivy missing before they reached the bike.

The going was slow as he pushed through the undergrowth, sometimes having to cut away vines and brush to pass. When he came within sight of the first shanty, he stopped and parked the motorcycle in the brush, memorizing the location by noting the tall tree with the Y fork at ten feet up.

"Connected with the DEA agents," Merlin said softly into Duff's headset. "So far, only women with donkey carts have come or gone from the compound. No vehicles have departed since they arrived in the night."

"Roger," Duff responded. "Moving closer."

The team had identified their fields of fire, or in this case, fields of observation.

Duff moved around to the far side of the compound, careful not to make noise in the brush. As he went, he looked for posted guards.

"Bogey at the eleven o'clock," Zip reported. "Armed with an AK-47."

"Bogey at nine o'clock," Woof announced. "AR 15 and enough ammo to start a war."

As Duff passed the back, opposite of the entrance, he spotted a guard leaning against a tree, his weapon slung over his shoulder. He had a rag in hand, mopping the sweat from his face.

"Guard at six o'clock," Duff said softly. "AR 15 rifle. Lots of magazines." He kept moving around to the other side of the little village of shacks made up of tin and plywood.

Another guard at the three o'clock sat in the dirt, his back against a tree, scraping a wicked knife across a long thin walking stick.

"Bogey at three o'clock," he reported. He moved closer to better see into the village.

The other structures were also plywood and tin shacks. He could make out the corners of a stucco wall surrounding a larger, more permanent building at the center of the village.

Women moved around the shacks, stirring pots of food over open fires and tending to children. Men carrying rifles and multiple magazines filled with bullets walked among them.

"Lots of civilians," Duff murmured into his mic."

"That's why we wait until dark to make our move," Merlin's voice stated calmly. "Hold steady."

Duff settled into position, watching the guard whittling on his walking stick, studying the compound, wishing he could make a move sooner than nightfall. They had no idea what was happening inside the stucco walls. Were they torturing Ivy? Was she in pain?

Duff's hands bunched into fists. The waiting was the worst part of any mission. He told himself to use the time to study everything about the layout and people he could see moving around. The last thing they wanted to do was incur civilian casualties extracting the senator's daughter.

But, damn it, he had to get her out alive.

CHAPTER 13

IVY WAS HALFWAY out the window when she heard the key in the lock behind her. From what she could tell, the sun had passed its zenith and was headed down, casting shadows on the little alley between the building she was in and another. At the end of the alley was a six-foot-high wall. How she'd get over it, she had no idea.

First, she had to get out of the room before whoever was at the door entered and noticed she wasn't where she was supposed to be.

With no other choice, she wiggled and squirmed until her hips were through. She dropped down, headfirst, her arms outstretched to catch her fall.

She landed hard on one hand, twisting her wrist. Pain shot through it. She swallowed a moan. A twisted wrist wouldn't slow her down. Ivy rolled over, bunched her legs beneath her, and leaped to her feet.

A door slammed open in the room she'd just vacated, and a shout sounded.

The alarm went up. Men yelled inside the building and more outside.

Her escape would be short-lived if she didn't make it out of the compound before the entire army of cartel thugs were aware of what all the shouting was about.

She ran to the end of the alley. The wall extended to the left and right. She guessed it was a walled compound and this barrier stood between her and freedom. She had to find a way over it, or she'd be caught, returned to her prison, and beaten for her attempt to escape.

Ivy turned right and ran along the barricade, praying she'd find something to climb up on. She came across another alleyway. In that alley was a stack of wooden pallets.

She grabbed one, lugged it over to the wall and leaned it against the stucco. The pallet's slats acted like a ladder, allowing her to climb high enough to get her arms over the top of the wall and pull herself up and over. She winced at the pain in her wrist but powered through.

As footsteps pounded around the corner of the building she'd just left, Ivy rolled over the edge of the wall and dropped to the ground on the other side.

Men shouted inside the walls and more shouted back in what appeared to be a poor village surrounding the stucco compound. Her breath caught in her throat and her chest tightened. Based on the language and the squalor around her, she guessed she wasn't in the US.

No matter. Most countries in the world had US Embassies. She'd find this country's embassy and seek sanctuary there.

Ivy raced for one of the small huts and hid beside it in the shadows cast by the setting sun.

Women grabbed up small children and ran into the nearby jungle.

Men carrying military-grade rifles raced past where she hid in the shadows. When they disappeared between still more shacks, Ivy peered around the corner and made a run for the next building, leapfrogging from the shadows of one shack to the next, working her way toward the edge of the village.

For a weapon, she snatched up a log sticking out of a fire pit. One end had yet to catch fire, the other smoldered, the outside covered in ash, the inside burning with hot coals.

In her next leap to another shack's cover, Ivy wasn't as lucky. She nearly ran into a man running toward the compound. They didn't see each other until the last moment.

As he recognized her, the man raised his rifle.

Acting on instinct, Ivy swung the log, hitting him in the face with the smoldering end.

He screeched, dropped his weapon and clutched his face.

Ivy ran past him. She had to get to the jungle. Recapture was not an option. Guayabera Man wouldn't be so lenient with her next time.

She had reached the last hut when the entire village seemed to be heading her way. Shots were fired—at what, she had no idea, nor was she planning to stick around to find out. With nowhere else to go, she had to make the dash across the open ground between the village and the jungle.

Taking a deep breath, she raced out into the open.

A man stepped out of the shadows, wearing dark clothes and carrying an AK-47. He leveled the weapon at her chest and shouted in Spanish. *"¡Detener! O te dispararé!"*

Ivy didn't understand the words, but his intent was clear. If she didn't stop, he'd shoot her.

She gritted her teeth, her fists clenching. The bastard would have to shoot her. She wasn't stopping and she wasn't going back to that little cell to be beaten. She picked up her pace and ran straight at the man with the gun. If he shot her, at least she wouldn't suffer at the hands of Guayabera Man. If he missed, she had a chance of getting away.

The man yelled again, leveled his weapon at her and pulled the trigger.

Ivy braced for impact. When she didn't feel the pain of a bullet ripping through her chest, she slowed and looked down, then back up again.

The man was fiddling with his weapon. It hadn't gone off. She hadn't been shot.

Hope gave her feet wings. She thought about slamming into the man, knocking him off his feet so that he had more than a malfunctioning gun to worry about.

He worked frantically to unjam his weapon as Ivy neared him.

At the last moment, she dodged the man and kept running, lifting her knees and elbows, running as fast as she could toward the shadows of the trees just a few more feet away.

Behind her, she heard a shout. *"¡Detener!"*

A glance over her shoulder made her blood freeze in her veins.

Five men ran out of the village, carrying semi-automatic weapons, all aimed at her.

She dove for the shadows as gunfire erupted around her.

Once in the shadows, she crawled toward the trunk of a tree, keeping as low to the ground as possible, to make less of a target.

Winded, she reached the tree, out of breath and without sustaining any wounds. With what little strength she had left, she rolled behind the trunk where she paused to suck air into her lungs.

The gunfire continued around her. When she dared look around the tree again, the five men were lying on the ground. Three of them lay still, their guns lying in the dirt beside them. The other two lay in prone positions, their weapons pointed in her direction, shooting until they ran out of bullets.

When the gunfire ceased momentarily, Ivy pushed to her feet and made a run for it, heading deeper into the woods. She'd rather face hostile wildlife than the men who'd captured her and brought her to this village in the woods. She didn't know where she was or where she was going, but anywhere was better than where she'd been.

She ran as fast as her feet could carry her, praying it was fast enough to get her out of range of the bullets flying out behind her.

DUFF SAW Ivy as soon as she cleared the shadows of the shack on the outskirts of the village.

How the hell she'd gotten loose was a mystery, but she was in grave danger. The guard he'd been watching had finished whittling his walking stick and was moving toward the village at the same time as Ivy made her bid for escape.

As Duff watched in horror, the guard raised his weapon and aimed it at Ivy.

Duff couldn't get a bead on the man without the possibility of missing and hitting Ivy instead. All he could do was watch in disbelief as the guard aimed at the woman Duff could be falling in love with.

Instead of dropping to the ground, Ivy ran full tilt at the guard.

Is she insane?

Duff aimed at the guard, waiting for the moment Ivy would drop to the ground and give him a clear shot.

The guard stiffened.

From Duff's vantage point, he could see the guard's arm tighten. He could almost feel the man pulling the trigger.

For a moment, Duff's heart hit the pit of his belly. He waited for the surprised look on Ivy's face, the patch of blood that would spread on her shirt, and for her to clutch her hand to her chest and fall to the ground.

When she didn't, he squinted.

Had the man missed?

The guard looked down at his weapon, tapped the magazine, pulled back the bolt and tapped the magazine again.

The gun had jammed.

Duff's heart made the leap from the bottom of his gut to his throat. "Run," he whispered. "Ivy. Run."

"What's going on, Duff?" Merlin asked.

"Ivy's made her escape. She's on the edge of the camp, facing off with one of the guards."

"Shoot him," Woof said.

"Can't," Duff said. "Ivy's in direct line of fire. If I miss, I could hit her. If I hit him, the bullet could pass through him and hit her." Though he couldn't shoot, he could take the guy from behind with his knife.

Ivy saved him from that decision when she dodged the guard and made a beeline toward the shadowy jungle.

She'd almost made it when men emerged from the edge of the village and shouted in Spanish for Ivy to stop.

"Don't stop," Duff murmured. He put the drop on the man with the jammed gun and then set his sights on the lead man of the guys who'd just emerged from the village. The lead raised his AR-15, aiming at Ivy. "Five bogeys going after Ivy. Could use some fire support."

"On it," Zip said. "Coming in from the compound's two o'clock."

"In the brush at the three o'clock," Duff said. "Don't shoot me."

"Don't worry," Zip said. "You're a hard one to mistake for anyone else."

Duff looked down his sights at the leader, raising his weapon to aim at Ivy's back as she ran for the tree line.

When the cartel member aimed his rifle at her, Duff pulled the trigger, hitting him square in the chest. The man dropped where he stood.

Before the guy beside him could get a bead on Ivy, Duff took him out as well.

Ivy dove into the brush and lay flat on the ground.

Another shot was fired from Duff's right, taking out a third man. The other two dropped to the ground and turned their weapons on Duff and Zip.

Duff aimed low. The men lay so near to the ground, they were practically invisible in the impending gloom of dusk.

Duff waited for one of them to move to get a clear shot.

A second passed, then two.

A shadow on the ground moved just enough, allowing Duff to pick him out of the low-lying brush. He aimed, pulled the trigger and watched as the man jerked and then lay so still, he could only be dead.

The other man turned and low-crawled back to the shanties and disappeared in between the buildings.

"We need to get out of here," Duff said. "I'll get Ivy. Cover me."

"Got your back, brother," Zip said.

Duff circled around in the brush, moving quietly from shadow to shadow until he maneuvered into position several feet away from where Ivy still lay against the ground, her head down, her body trembling.

Duff watched the edge of the village for more

men to pop out and start shooting. When none came immediately, he rushed forward.

About that time, several men ran out of the village, firing toward them.

Duff raced toward Ivy and threw himself on top of her.

She grunted and then struggled beneath him, kicking her feet, trying to roll over to fight back.

Ivy battled fiercely, jamming an elbow into Duff's side and reaching back to pinch his neck when he leaned over her.

"Hey," he whispered into her hear. "It's me. Duff."

Her body stilled. "Duff?"

"Yeah, sweetheart, it's me." He dropped a kiss on the back of her neck as they stood. "Ready to get the hell out of here?"

She nodded. "Yes."

"Then come with me." He held out his hand. "Stick to the shadows. Zip's providing cover."

"Thank God," she said and leaned into him. "How did you find me?" she asked.

"Long story. We can talk later. First things first. We need to get you back to civilization.

She nodded. "Lead the way. I'll follow."

"No. You need to go in front of me."

"So you can block the bullets?" She shook her head. "I don't want you to put yourself in harm's way to take a bullet for me."

"Too late, sweetheart. At least on the harm's way.

Your chariot awaits on the other side of this compound. The only ways to get there are to go straight through or make a wide berth of the entire village."

"I'm game to take the long way around," she said. "Not fond of the people who held me captive."

"I've got your six. You're not going back to them," Duff reassured her. "Let's go."

To his teammates, he announced, "Taking the long road home."

"We'll keep them occupied until you give us the all-clear," Merlin said.

"Roger," Duff said. He took Ivy's hand in his and swung wide of the compound and the other members of his team, staying hunkered low to the ground, moving in the shadows as night settled in on the village.

Gunfire sounded as his team kept the cartel members guessing which direction they could move.

The Deltas wouldn't just fire into the camp. Not with the possibility of hitting innocent women and children. They'd fire over the top. If one of the cartel members came within range and presented a threat, Merlin and the others would eliminate the problem.

Meanwhile, Duff and Ivy hurried around the perimeter. The jungle was different in the dark. Duff almost passed his landmark without realizing it. At the last moment, he looked up as he stood beneath the tree with the Y fork in it.

His pulse kicked up a notch. They were going to make it out of the jungle and back to civilization. He would have a chance at another date with this incredible woman who'd managed to get away from a notoriously vicious cartel. He wanted to hear that story. But, it would have to wait until they got to safety.

Pulling the leaves and brush away from where he'd stashed his motorcycle, Duff mounted and made room for her on the back. "You're gonna have to hold on really tight. We won't be taking the road out of here. That will be the first place they'll look for us."

"You sure you know which way to go in this jungle?" she asked.

He nodded. "I'll follow the road without getting up on it. If we see signs of the cartel following us, we'll go deeper.

She nodded. "Let's do this."

He touched his hand to her cheek. "I want to hear your story on how you escaped."

"Don't worry. I'll tell you...later," she promised. "Where are we, anyway?"

He grinned in the darkness, his teeth shining brightly in the gloom. "Costa Rica."

"Costa Rica?" she repeated. "Holy hell."

As soon as Ivy mounted the motorcycle, Duff started the engine, put the bike in gear, and took off, headed south toward Cahuita. He hated leaving his team behind to fight the well-armed cartel members without his help. But the whole reason they'd come to Costa Rica was to find and rescue Ivy Fremont. He needed to get her as far away from the cartel camp as possible.

He rode through the jungle, running parallel with the road, operating the bike with the lights out. Their movement was a lot slower than he would have liked, but the canopy of leaves above effectively blocked what little light was emitted from the stars shining down.

He'd like nothing more than to hop up onto the road and open the throttle, racing away from the camp, the cartel, and anyone else who wanted to shoot at them.

They couldn't ride out in the open in case the cartel caught up with them or notified other members farther along the highway to be on the lookout for their escaped hostage.

After fifteen minutes of dodging logs, trees, and underbrush, Duff's shoulders were tense, and his hands already ached on the handlebars. It would be a very long ride if he had to do it all in the jungle.

Lights ahead on the road made him slow to a stop. Duff ran the motorcycle back behind the trees and parked.

Ivy got off the back. Duff dismounted and worked his way through the trees toward the road.

Ivy followed, staying low and moving in the shadows.

As the headlights neared, Ivy and Duff ducked low in the bushes and watched.

A truckload of men bearing guns raced past, headed for the compound.

Duff swore softly.

Ivy touched a hand to his shoulder. "I hope your teammates will be all right."

"They will be," he said, praying he was right. He wanted all the men to return home.

"You want to go back and help, don't you?" she said.

He squared his shoulders. "No. My job is to get you to safety. Theirs is to provide the distraction so that I can do my job."

When the truck's taillights disappeared down the road, Duff took her hand and walked with her back to the motorcycle. He pulled her into his arms and kissed her hard on the mouth. "I didn't know if I'd get to do that again."

She sighed and leaned into him. "I didn't know if you lived through that fall over the cliff."

"I've done worse off that cliff and lived."

He couldn't see her expression in the dark, just the whites of her eyes and teeth.

"Come on, we have a long way to go before morning."

"Where are we going?"

"To our rendezvous point."

"And that is?"

"The coast."

"How far?"

"Depends on how heavily monitored the roads are. Normally, it would take maybe a little more than an hour. Since there are so few roads leading in and out of the interior, we're limited to this one."

"Better safe than sorry." She waited for him to climb on the back of the motorcycle and then slipped on behind him. "Have I told you how glad I am that you survived that fall?"

He covered her hand with his for a brief moment. Duff leaned back so that he could see her silhouette in the darkness. "I'm glad we found you. Had you not been wearing the necklace your mother gave you, we wouldn't have known where to begin. Did you know it contained a tracking device?"

Her hand rose to her neck. "My necklace! It's gone. And no. Mother didn't tell me that little secret. She only told me that my father had meant to give it to me before he died, and that I should always wear it to remember him. And I have."

"She must love you a lot to embed a GPS tracking disk inside it." Duff slipped his hand into her pocket and pulled out the necklace, handing it to her. "We found it on the tarmac at the airport in Killeen, tracked the plane that had just left for Costa Rica, and had agents on the ground watching for when it landed in Limón."

She slipped the chain over her head and tucked

the pendent beneath her blouse. "Thank you. All this time I only considered the thought that it was my father's wish for me to wear it." She pressed her hand over her blouse and the pendant. "I guess my mother really does care about me, more than just trying to run my life." She smiled in the darkness, her white teeth the only thing he could tell by.

She wrapped her arms around his neck and leaned up to kiss his cheek. "Thank you for coming to my rescue."

"Don't thank me yet. Not until we have you back on US soil." His lips twitched as he recalled seeing her run out of the village and straight at the guard holding a gun on her. "If I recall, you were on your way to rescuing yourself." He still had heart palpitations from the moment the guard pulled the trigger and the gun jammed. Ivy's number had obviously not been up.

They took off again, bumping along the side of the road, sometimes riding down the center, but mostly staying off-road to avoid unseen sentries waiting for them to pass.

It must have been near midnight when they approached a quiet village somewhere between the compound and Cahuita. Duff recalled seeing the village on the map.

He switched off the motorcycle engine and let it glide to a stop at the side of the road.

They dismounted on the edge of the little town of

huts and a few concrete block buildings. Several lightbulbs burned in the darkness illuminating the area at the center of the settlement. Beneath the lights stood a couple of men smoking cigarettes and carrying military-grade rifles.

"We'll walk it around the village," he whispered. "The less noise we make the less likely they'll spot us."

Duff pushed the motorcycle through the trees outside the edges of the village. Ivy walked beside him.

They'd nearly made it to the other end of town when a stray dog barked. His bark got another one going until every dog in town was sending up the alarm.

Through the huts, Duff could see the men bearing arms looking left and right.

The stray dogs grouped together and raced toward where Duff and Ivy stood in the shadows of the trees.

"Time to ride," Duff said. He climbed onto the bike and started the engine as Ivy slid onto the seat behind him.

The dogs rushed out of the village straight for them.

Duff twisted the throttle, giving the lightweight bike a shot of fuel, sending them flying through the trees and out the other end of the village.

He didn't look back. They had only a few seconds before the sentries got in whatever vehicle they had and came after them. Those few seconds meant the difference between getting away or being caught.

Duff was leaning toward the scenario where they got away.

"I see headlights behind us," Ivy shouted into his ear.

Duff gave the bike the full throttle and hopped out of the trees onto the road. They wouldn't get away if they didn't get some distance between them and the pursuing vehicles before they ducked back into the trees to hide.

He raced down the road, kicking up dust behind them. They'd gone a couple of miles when the road dipped down into a small stream. Someone had poured concrete over the road to make it a permanent low-water crossing.

Duff slowed and drove down into the water, then turned and headed downstream, driving in the middle of the bed, kicking up water on both sides. Several yards downstream, he drove up into a tributary and out of the water onto the bank, heading back the way they'd come.

He turned back toward the road and stopped while still deep in the foliage and shut down the engine.

Still seated on the motorcycle, Ivy's arms wrapped around his waist, he waited.

CHAPTER 14

When the headlights appeared on the road, Ivy held her breath, her heart pounding so hard, she was sure Duff could feel it where her chest pressed against his back.

The closer the lights came, the tighter she held on to Duff's waist.

She didn't want to go back to the compound.

Duff had stopped the motorcycle behind a stand of trees and low-lying brush. They could barely see the headlights through the brush. Hopefully, the men in the vehicle wouldn't see them.

As the vehicle passed, Ivy could see that it appeared to be an old Jeep with the top removed and a machine gun mounted in the center, manned by a rough-looking cartel member. On either side in the back seat were two more men, both carrying semi-automatic rifles with banana clips.

Ivy willed herself, Duff and the motorcycle to be invisible to the heavily armed men. If they even *thought* Ivy and Duff were nearby, they might open fire and mow down everything in their path until they finally got to the compound escapees.

The Jeep continued down the road, dipping down into the low-water crossing and back up on the other side. They didn't stop or turn back but kept moving.

"Where to now?" Ivy asked.

"We wait," Duff said. "They'll be back when they don't catch up with us."

They dismounted and crouched in the bushes. Ivy strained her eyes trying to see into the darkness. The stars shined down on the road where the canopy of trees didn't meet on either side.

For the next thirty minutes, they remained still in the brush, waiting for the men to return in their search for them.

Just as Duff predicted, the Jeep eventually returned, moving even slower than before.

Duff and Ivy ducked down as they passed by shining a high-beam spotlight into the shadows. Ivy counted bodies. Two side gunners, machine gunner and driver. They were all present and accounted for.

One of the men shouted.

The Jeep stopped.

Duff raised his weapon and pointed at the men, ready to open fire if they started toward their position.

Ivy's pulse pounded hard and she squatted lower to the ground.

One of the men slung his weapon over his shoulder, reached for his pants, unzipped and relieved himself on the side of the road.

When he was finished, he climbed back on the Jeep and it took off a little faster this time.

Ivy released the breath she'd been holding and swallowed hard to keep from laughing hysterically.

When the taillights disappeared around a curve in the road, Duff stood. "Let's go. It won't be long before sunrise and we need to be at our destination before daylight."

He mounted the motorcycle. Ivy climbed on behind him and leaned against him. They drove down the center of the road away from the village and hopefully toward the coast.

The drugs they'd used on her and the stress she was under dragged at Ivy, making her sleepy. She couldn't succumb or she'd fall off the back of the bike.

Duff hadn't come all that way to rescue her only to have her die because she fell off the back of the motorcycle.

She fought to stay awake, holding tightly to Duff, feeling as safe as she could possibly be in a hostile environment.

Eventually, they came to another town, this one bigger than the village.

The road changed from gravel and dirt to pavement.

Before they entered, Duff ditched his HK 416 and his vest with the extra magazines, burying them beneath a fallen, rotting tree trunk. He slid a magazine of 9mm bullets in one of the pockets of his cargo pants. He tucked the 9mm Glock in the other pant pocket. The last thing he pulled was the communications device out of his ear, stuffing it into his front pocket.

By the time he was finished, he looked like any tourist on a driving tour of the beautiful country of Costa Rica. After marking the GPS location on his phone, he climbed back on the motorcycle and waited for Ivy to slide on behind him.

As soon as they entered the town, Duff turned off the main road and zigzagged through the narrow streets.

This town was more affluent. Beautiful homes were adorned with climbing bougainvillea. The rich and vibrantly colored flowers made a sharp contrast to the stark white stucco. Between some of the homes, Ivy caught glimpses of the starlight glinting off water.

Duff slowed in a back alley, pulled out his cellphone and brought up an app with a map and a preloaded address. Based on the little blue dot noting their current location, they weren't far from their destination.

And a place I can lay down and sleep, Ivy thought.

"Let me hold the phone," she said.

He handed it to her. She held it in front of him where he could check it at the street corners as he drove through the streets. When they finally arrived at the address he'd loaded, they pulled in front of a tall stucco wall with an iron gate. He took the phone from her and called a number.

"Vance? Magnus McCormick. Sorry to call you so early." He paused. "Actually, I need a favor. Remember you said whenever I was in Costa Rica to look you up?" Again, he paused. "Well, I'm here… outside your gate. Mind if we come in?"

All the while Duff was on the call, Ivy stared around the neighborhood, paranoia tugging at her tired mind. The sun had yet to rise, but the gray light of predawn made it easy for them to see and be seen. She prayed Duff's friend would hurry and let them in.

A moment later, a man in a pair of swim shorts and sandals, his hair standing on end from having just risen from his bed, opened the gate and pushed the wrought iron rails wide. "Come in, come in," he said and waved them through.

Duff pushed the motorcycle out of the street and into the courtyard. "Got a place we can stash this where no one will see it? We have people looking for us."

Vance's eyes widened. "People?"

"Not exactly sure, but we think we pissed off members of a cartel. And for the matter, we understand if you don't want us to stay."

Vance shook his head. "No, no. Please, get inside. I have a shed in the back where you can store the bike." He led the way around the white stucco house to the shed, passing pots of red geraniums and bright pink oleander bushes.

Ivy's tired brain struggled to make the connection to the vacation atmosphere of the home and the harshness of the cartel compound in the jungle. It was as if they'd traveled to an entirely different country when they arrived in the town.

Once Duff had the bike stored out of sight, Vance led them through the back door of his home into a bright, clean, modern kitchen with everything a chef could want to cook up anything the owner's heart desired.

"Nice place," Duff said.

"Thanks. I like it. Year-round sunshine and tropical breezes beat North Carolina's humid summers and cold winters any day."

"Vance," Duff turned to Ivy. "This is my girlfriend, Amy Smith. Amy, Vance Tate. Vance and I met six years ago in a bar we frequented outside Fort Bragg, North Carolina when I was stationed there."

"And we kept in touch ever since." Vance held out his hand to Duff first.

Duff gripped his hand.

Vance pulled him in for a hug. "We played a few rounds of sand volleyball at that bar. We were a pair. No one could beat us."

Duff nodded. "Many tried."

Vance let go of Duff's hand and reached for Ivy's. "Amy, you said?"

Ivy glanced at Duff before answering, "That's right. Amy Smith."

"Nice to meet you, Amy. About time Magnus found him a woman. You must be special if he finally succumbed to the fairer sex."

"I don't know about that, but he's pretty special to me," she said and meant it.

"What happened to your face, my dear?" Vance asked.

She brushed the hair to the side, exposing the cut at her temple. "I hit a branch going through the woods getting away from those people we pissed off."

Duff frowned. "We need to take care of that before it gets infected."

"There's a bathroom in the bedroom off the corridor to the right. I'll grab the first aid kit."

Duff led the way down a hallway to a bedroom with a white iron bed and white lace curtains floating in the breeze through the window. He entered the room and turned to her, studying her face. His lips pressed into a thin line. "I didn't know you were hurt." He took her hand, drew her into the bathroom, and turned on the water.

"It's nothing," she said, holding the hair out of her face while he dabbed a clean wet washrag over the cut.

"Those bastards do this to you?" he asked, his mouth so close to hers she had only to rise up on her toes to brush her lips to his.

"Guayabera Man wanted me to make a video to send to my mother. I refused." She shrugged. "He hit me and made me make the video."

"Wish I had known that," Duff said.

"What could you have done?" Ivy said.

His jaw hardened. "I could have killed him." He pulled her into his arms and held her.

"It doesn't matter now," she whispered against his chest.

"Here's the first aid kit," Vance appeared in the doorway. "I also grabbed some shorts and T-shirts you can wear if you'd like to shower and change. I can have the maid wash your clothes and return them to you when they're dry."

Ivy stepped back. "Thank you. I'd love a shower."

"You're welcome to use the facilities and have use of this bedroom while you're here. If you need anything else, I'll be in the kitchen. I'll wake the maid and have her prepare some food. You're bound to be hungry if you've been on the road all night."

"Oh, please, don't go to any trouble," Ivy said.

"No trouble," Vance said. "I was about to get up

anyway. I like to go down to the beach for a morning swim. I'll just do it after breakfast."

Duff finished cleaning Ivy's wound and applied an antiseptic ointment and a bandage. Then he pressed a gentle kiss to her forehead.

Ivy chuckled. "Kissing my booboo?"

"No. I'm kissing my girlfriend." He pulled her into his arms and gave her a real kiss.

"I'd really like to take advantage of the shower before I even attempt to eat anything. They gave me something to put me out for the plane ride here. I'm not sure what it was, but I woke with a headache."

"Do you need any help?" Duff asked.

A slow smile tilted Ivy's lips. "Need? Maybe not. Want? Yes." She nodded toward the door. "Gonna close that?"

DUFF KICKED it shut with his foot and reached around her to turn on the water in the shower.

Ivy reached for the hem of his shirt and dragged it up over his head, dropping it to the tiled floor.

He hooked his fingers in the ribbed knit shirt she wore and pulled it off in one smooth move, letting it fall on top of his shirt.

Ivy unhooked the front of her bra and let it slide off her shoulders.

Duff's gaze met hers. "I didn't bring protection."

"You've heard of withdrawal before release?"

she asked as she unbuttoned the rivet at her waistband, kicked off her shoes and shimmied out of her jeans and panties. She stepped free and kicked them aside, standing naked in front of him. "But if that doesn't work, we have other options."

Duff stripped in seconds, scooped her up into his arms and carried her into the walk-in shower with glass bricks and marble tiles.

He dipped beneath the spray with her in his arms, letting the water splash over their heads and down their backs.

She laughed and leaned her head back, rubbed shampoo into her hair, letting the water wash away the dust from the road. Ivy applied conditioner and rubbed it into the tangles. "You just applied a bandage."

"There were more," he said, and set her on her feet. He squirted bodywash into his palm and smoothed it over her shoulders and arms, loving how soft her skin was beneath his fingertips.

Ivy guided his hands to her breasts where he swirled the suds around her nipples, making them harden into tight little buttons.

She sucked in a deep breath, the motion pushing her chest out, giving him full range of her breasts.

He turned her to the side, letting the water wash away the soap. Then he bent to take one nipple into his mouth, sucking hard. He flicked it with his tongue and then moved to take the other nipple, rolling it between his teeth.

Ivy moaned and wove her fingers into his hair, pulling him closer.

He sucked, flicked and nibbled until the tension was so tight inside him, he couldn't wait any longer. Duff lifted her by the backs of her thighs, pressed her back to the tiles and nudged her entrance with the tip of his shaft. "Are you sure?"

She nodded. "Yes," she said and lowered herself over him.

He pushed up into her.

Her channel tightened around him.

"You feel so good," he murmured into her ear.

"Move," she said in a tight voice. "I want it fast and hard."

Holding her hips, he pressed her into the wall and pumped in and out of her, holding tightly to his control. Again and again, he thrust.

She rode him, her hands on his shoulders, her legs locked at the ankles behind him.

When he could hold out no longer, he lifted her off him and set her on her feet.

She took hold of his staff in both hands and finished what they'd started. He came in an explosion of sensations that left him pulsing with the intensity.

The shower water was cooling when he drew in a deep breath and let it out. "Your turn," he said, advancing on her.

She shook her head. "Your friend will be waiting to feed us breakfast."

"You'd rather have breakfast than an orgasm?" He cocked an eyebrow.

She started to nod her head and then shook it instead.

He turned her back to the showerhead and dropped to his knees.

She gasped. "What are you doing?"

"Giving you an orgasm," he said. "Concentrate," he demanded.

He parted her folds and dipped his finger into her moist channel. God, she felt good. He could feel himself harden all over again. But this wasn't about getting him off. He wanted her to feel what he'd felt.

Adding a second and a third finger, he slid in and out of her. Then he leaned in and flicked that nubbin of flesh that set her on fire.

She gasped and grabbed his hair.

He chuckled and flicked his tongue again, tapping the tip of her clit, then swirling it around and around.

Her body tensed and she rose on her toes. "Oh, baby," she whispered. "There. There."

He tongued, teased, and flicked her there until she was pulling hard on his hair and her fingers dug into his scalp.

He didn't care. She was riding the wave and he couldn't stop until she shot the curl to the end.

She cried out his name and stiffened, her breathing arrested, her muscles tight. Then she pumped her hips, faster and faster, her body writhing.

When she finally sagged in the cool water, she drew in a long breath, hooked her hands beneath his arms, and dragged him to his feet. "Who needs to eat, when you can have that?" She kissed him, wrapping a leg around the back of his thigh, rubbing her sex against his muscle.

Yeah, he could do it again. He was hard enough, but their host was waiting.

Duff kissed her hard and then set her to arm's length, reaching behind her to turn off the shower that had gone cold, not that they'd noticed until then.

He stepped out of the shower, grabbed a large fluffy white towel and rubbed her body from top to bottom.

Ivy took another towel and dried him off, pausing at his engorged cock. "Want to do something about that?"

"You know I do. But as you pointed out, our host will be waiting."

"After breakfast," she said with a wink. "Is it too soon to go to bed?"

"Not for people who've been up all night." He kissed her ear and tossed her a T-shirt and a pair of men's shorts.

She pulled the shirt over her head and let it fall

down around her hips. The hem reached to the middle of her thighs. She didn't really need the shorts as the shirt was as good as any dress. But she pulled them on since her panties would be going to the laundry with the rest of her clothing.

When they were both dressed in the shirts and shorts Vance had provided, Duff replaced the damp bandage with a fresh, dry one. Then they padded down the hallway in their bare feet to the kitchen.

Vance stood beside a pretty, dark-haired maid, a cellphone in his hand.

When he saw them at the doorway to the kitchen, he ended his call and smiled. "There you are. I'm glad you took advantage of the shower. Being on the road all night, especially some of our dusty roads, leaves you gritty and sticky. Come have a seat at the table. Angela has prepared some American favorites: scrambled eggs, bacon and toast."

Duff held a chair for Ivy and waited until she sat before he took the seat beside her.

Vance settled in the one across from Ivy. "So, where did you start your journey last night? I can't imagine driving on a motorcycle through the night in Costa Rica. The roads can be dangerous in some areas."

Duff reached for the scrambled eggs and spooned a portion onto his plate. He passed them to Ivy. "Do you have many problems in Costa Rica?" he asked.

Vance lifted his shoulders and took the platter of

eggs from Ivy. "As much as you would expect. Costa Rica is between Columbia and the US. You would expect some corruption by the cartels who run illegal product to their buyers in the US."

"How do you stay clear of the cartels?"

"Some people pay protection fees," Vance said. "Others do favors for the cartels to keep them off their backs. Not everyone is impacted by the cartels. Most tourist cities rarely see the cartel's activities. Unless one of the tourists succumbs to the lure of quick money to fund the movement of drugs."

"It's a shame that the cartels have so much sway in the communities," Ivy said.

"What about you, Amy? What do you do back in the States?" Vance asked.

"I run a gift shop." She smiled. "I don't make much, but I like what I do."

Vance leaned forward. "Tell me...if you had the opportunity to make a lot more money, would you take it?"

Ivy frowned. "I did have an opportunity to make a lot more money, but I purposely chose not to."

"Why?" Vance asked.

"It wasn't worth the way I felt afterward. I didn't like what I was doing, I didn't like myself." She shook her head. "I'm poorer, but happier."

He nodded. "I understand that."

"Is that why you moved to Costa Rica?" Duff asked. "I understand the cost of living is better here."

"Partly." Vance raised his arms out wide. "And who could resist paradise?"

When they finished their meal, Ivy offered to help with the dishes.

"Don't. Angela does all the housework. It's her job." When Ivy would have protested, Vance stopped her with, "You wouldn't want to deprive her of a paycheck, would you?"

"No, of course not," she said and yawned.

"I was about to ask if you wanted a tour of our lovely city, but I think you two might be more in need of rest after your all-night ride through the jungle."

Ivy smiled. "That would be nice. I could stand to take a short nap."

"Please, make yourselves at home," Vance said. "We can catch up later when you're well-rested."

"Thanks, Vance," Duff said. "We appreciate your hospitality. You were always a good sport. I miss the old days of hanging out at the bar, playing volleyball in their sand court with you."

Vance's smile slipped. "I miss the old, simpler days as well." His smile returned. "Now, please, get some sleep. I'll be here when you wake."

"Thank you," Ivy said, preceding Duff down the hall to the bedroom.

Once inside, Duff closed the door and twisted the lock on the handle. "As much as I like making love to you…"

"...I would rather sleep as well." She smiled and laid down on her side on the bed, bunching the pillow beneath her chin.

Duff entered the bathroom and gathered his cargo pants, leaving the rest for the maid to wash. He pulled the radio headset out of his front pocket and slipped it in his ear. He carried the handgun to the bed and slipped it beneath his pillow before he laid down facing Ivy.

"Think the cartel will find us here?" Ivy asked.

"It doesn't hurt to be ready if they do."

"What's next?" she asked with another yawn, her eyelids drifting closed.

He smoothed her damp hair back from her forehead. "We wait to hear from our ride home." He pulled her into his embrace and held her as she drifted off to sleep.

He remained awake longer, hoping he'd been right to bring her to Vance's place. He wondered if they should have waited on the edge of town or checked into a hotel under a different name.

Before he closed his eyes for a short nap, he whispered into his headset. "Merlin? You there, buddy?"

CHAPTER 15

A SOUND WOKE IVY, penetrating a shallow sleep filled with nightmares about Guayabera Man standing over her, swinging his fat hand at her face.

The sound came again. That of car doors slamming and footsteps running.

She sat up in the bed and looked for Duff.

He was coming out of the bathroom, carrying their dirty clothing. "Get your shoes on."

Her pulse beat hard and fast. He hadn't said it, but he meant for her to hurry.

While he opened the window wide, she shoved her feet into her hiking boots and laced them halfway up, not wanting to take more time than she had to. She was on her feet and standing beside him as he shoved his gun into the pocket of the cargo pants he'd put on over the shorts.

"What's going on?" she whispered.

"I'm not sure, but I heard voices outside. One of them was Vance, talking to someone else in Spanish." He lifted her over the windowsill and dropped her onto her feet outside. "Run to the back wall. I'll be right behind you.

She hesitated.

"Go," he urged, then turned and grabbed a chair from the desk in the corner and jammed it beneath the door handle.

Ivy understood and did as he'd said, running to the back wall where she looked for anything she could use to scale the wall. No pallets were lying around, but she did find a five-gallon empty paint bucket. She turned it upside down, stepped onto it and pulled herself up onto the wall, lying flat against the stucco to avoid detection.

From her vantage point, she could see into the alley. So far, nothing moved there but a stray cat. Looking toward the front of the house, she could just see around the corner to the front. A dark SUV was parked there. As she watched, a Jeep pulled up behind it. A Jeep with a machinegun mounted in the middle and a man standing behind it, his hand on the trigger.

Ivy's heart lodged in her throat. She flattened herself even more and scooted back, out of sight of the Jeep.

Duff squeezed his big body out the window and dropped to the ground. As big as he was, his footsteps made no sound as he ran toward her.

She pressed a finger to her lips and pointed toward the front of the house, then she slipped off the wall and landed on the other side.

Duff followed her, sliding over the top like a wraith, quiet, in control and ready for anything. He took her hand and they ran together to the end of the alley. There, he stopped and peered around the corner toward the street where the vehicles had parked.

"Clear," he said, and turned away from the house and the street. They wound through the neighborhood of white stucco houses, toward the coast.

"Where are we going?"

"To the beach."

"Wouldn't it be better to hide in the jungle?" she said, running to keep up with him.

He didn't answer.

Ivy could hear him talking quietly to himself. "Merlin, you copy? Lefty? Zip? Woof? Anyone?" He kept running, calling the names of his Delta Force teammates as he went. "Merlin, now would be a good time to tell me you're here. Do you copy?"

A shout sounded behind them.

Ivy turned to see a man in black standing at the end of the street. He yelled and shook his fist. Then he lowered his weapon to the firing position.

The crack of gunfire rang out, echoing off the walls of the nice homes.

Duff grabbed Ivy's arm and yanked her to the

right, ducking into an alley. He kept running, bringing her along with him.

Her lungs burned and her muscles strained as she ran for her life. When she didn't think she could go another step, Duff ground to a halt. They were about two blocks from the water and the open beach. She had no desire to step out in the open and expose themselves to the man with the machinegun on the back of the Jeep.

Instead of continuing down to the water, Duff pulled her over a low wall and into the shadow of a gazebo in someone's backyard. Once there, he crouched low, cupped his hand over his ear where she could see an earbud, the two-way radio he'd worn the night before.

Duff's eyes narrowed and he spoke softly, urgently. "Merlin?"

Ivy knelt beside him, leaning close, hoping to hear whatever Duff might.

"Merlin, you copy?"

Ivy strained to hear anything. The sound of Merlin's voice in Duff's headset, the screech of brakes on a vehicle heading toward them, the crunch of footsteps on streets outside the wall they hid behind.

She used the time to fill her lungs and to will her heartbeat to return to a normal pace. When they started running again, she had to be ready. Duff could run so much faster and longer than she could.

But she refused to slow him down to the point he was killed because she couldn't keep up.

She liked him. A lot.

He was strong, brave and sexy as hell. They were in a resort town in Costa Rica. The terror they were facing couldn't be happening. This could not be the end for them. She had plans. Plans that included going out on another date with Duff. A date that didn't end with him being pushed over a cliff and her being kidnapped and taken to a foreign country.

Duff's hand shot out to grab her arm. He looked up, his gaze capturing hers. "Merlin? Thank God."

Ivy nearly cried at the brief flash of relief in Duff's face.

"We're approximately two blocks from the beach, but someone let the cartel know where we were holed up. I suspect it was my buddy, Vance." He said that last with a bite to his tone. "He must be working with the cartel." He paused and listened. "How long until you arrive? You're here?" He rose in a crouch and looked over the low wall toward the beach. "I see it. I don't know if we'll be able to make it across the beach. They're here and they're heavily armed."

"Okay. We'll move into position and wait for the fireworks before we make a run for the boat. Glad you all made it out. Yeah, we're okay. See you in a few. Out here."

Duff's gaze met hers. "We have to get closer."

"To the beach?" Ivy's gut clenched. "That's an

awful lot of open air to run through. Not to mention putting the tourists at risk."

He nodded. "The team is setting up a diversion. We need to blend in with the beachgoers. Come on, we have some shopping to do."

"Shopping? Are you crazy? There are armed men after us."

"All the more reason to find disguises." He winked and checked both directions over the wall. "Clear. Let's go." He gripped her hand and ran toward the beach and the stores that lined the waterfront. He located a beachwear shop with racks of swimsuits and sunglasses and slipped around the corner and inside.

"I don't have any money," she said. "My purse is in your motorcycle back in Texas.

"I have a credit card. Find what you need for a touristy day at the beach and put it on in the changing room. And do something to hide your hair. It's a dead giveaway. Make it fast. Merlin's diversion won't be long in the making."

Ivy ducked her head and shopped faster than she'd ever shopped in her life. She selected a one-piece suit, a sheer coverup, water shoes instead of flipflops, floppy hat and sunglasses. She entered the changing room beside Duff. "I'll only be a minute," she said.

"I'll wait for you," he said.

Moments later, she'd ditched her boots, jeans, the

T-shirt Vance had given her, and dressed in the suit, coverup, water shoes and sunglasses. She wound her auburn hair up and tucked it into the floppy hat. A glance at her image in the full-length mirror showed a different person from the one who'd walked into the shop. The hat and sunglasses hid the bruises and the cut on her temple and her hair. She could be any one of the tourists there for a day on the beautiful sandy beaches of Costa Rica.

"I'm ready," she said, and stepped out of the dressing room.

Duff was waiting outside the door, dressed in a loud pair of swim trunks in a bright blue, green and red tropical print. He wore a matching tropical shirt, an old man's fisherman hat and sunglasses.

Ivy chuckled. "You don't want to stand out at all, do you?"

"Nope," he said. "Just trying to fit in." He slung a tote bag over his arm. Ivy suspected his gun and extra bullets were what was weighing it down. "I'm all paid up, let's get you checked out and find a place to wait for our cue."

"Do you know what that cue might be?"

"I'll know it when I hear it," he said.

Ivy stepped up to the counter and let the clerk cut the tags off her items and ring them up. Duff paid while keeping a watch out the window for the cartel.

When they were finished, they walked out the door like any other couple on vacation.

As soon as they cleared the entrance, the Jeep with the machinegun rolled out onto the street, moving slowly, the driver and gunners looking in both directions.

Ivy froze, glad for the anonymity of the sunglasses to hide her frightened expression.

Duff curled his hand around hers and smiled at the sunshine. "It's a glorious day, isn't it darlin'?"

Ivy forced a matching smile. "Yes, it is, dear."

The men on board looked their direction but kept going.

The Jeep rolled by. As soon as they passed, Duff turned the opposite direction and led Ivy away.

Ivy fought hard to keep her gaze forward, though she wanted to look back and see if the cartel thugs had turned around and were pointing their weapons at them.

They'd gone a block when a dark SUV pulled out onto the beachfront road.

"I could be mistaken, but that SUV looks like the one that was parked in front of Vance's house when we left," she said.

As the vehicle rolled past, the passenger window lowered, revealing the occupant.

Vance Tate.

He looked at them, his eyes narrowing slightly before he looked ahead.

The SUV passed.

"Bastard," Duff muttered beneath his breath.

Softly, he spoke into his headset, "Merlin, it's getting hot out here. We could use that diversion about now."

No sooner had the words left his mouth when a loud explosion ripped through the air. Ivy turned back toward the sound to see fireworks shooting up into the air, bursting one after the other.

Duff leaned close to her. "That's our cue. See that boat at the end of that pier?"

She nodded.

"That's our ticket out of here." He tucked her hand through his arm and started across the street, across a boardwalk, and out onto the pier.

Ivy glanced over her shoulder.

The dark SUV had stopped and the men were getting out, carrying guns.

"Run!" Duff yelled.

CHAPTER 16

DUFF HELD tight to Ivy's hand as they raced to the end of the pier.

A long cigar boat waited there. Merlin, Woof, Zip, and Jangles, wearing similar attire to Duff, stood waiting for them, their weapons at the ready.

Gunfire behind them made Duff run faster. He prayed the attackers were far enough from the men who'd left the SUV that the bullets would fall short, but they still had to get away.

As they neared the boat, he shouted, "Jump!"

He waited for Ivy to do as he said.

She flew off the pier onto the boat. Woof caught her and fell back in his seat. Duff landed on the bottom of the boat and rolled to his feet, pulling his gun from the bottom of the tote he'd purchased.

The jet boat raced away from the pier as the men

from the SUV, including Vance Tate, ran toward them.

Merlin sent the boat shooting out into the water as far and as fast as he could in sixty seconds.

Soon, the pier and the people on it were but distant specks on the horizon.

Duff turned back to where Ivy was on the back seat of the cigar boat. Instead of sitting up, she was lying across the seat on her belly with Woof holding his hand to a wound on her side.

The blood rushed from Duff's head, leaving him feeling dizzy. He dropped to his knees beside Ivy. "Sweetheart, talk to me." He leaned in close to hear her over the engine.

She chuckled and winced. "I think I caught a bullet."

He smoothed a hand over her hair as it whipped her cheek in the wind.

The cigar boat slapped the waves as it raced toward Limón and the air transport waiting for them there.

"Someone get on the sat phone and arrange for an armed escort from the pier to the hospital," Duff called out.

"On it," Jangles said, pointing to the sat phone he held to his ear.

"Does this qualify as a war story?" Ivy asked. "I should have enlisted in the Army." She snorted. "That would have given my mother a coronary." She gave him a crooked smile. "Might just do that. Is there an age limit?"

"Yes, but you're still within the guidelines," Woof said.

A tear slipped from the corner of Ivy's eye.

Duff took her hand. "Does it hurt that bad?"

She shook her head. "I was thinking."

"That's dangerous," Duff teased, a knot lodging in his throat. "About what?"

"What if," she gulped and started again. "What if that bullet damaged something important?"

"The docs can fix you right up."

She squeezed his hand. "No, what if it damaged my ability…to have children?"

"Oh, baby, you're going to be all right."

"There's so many more things I want to know about you," she said, closing her eyes.

"Like what?"

"Do you like children?" she asked, her eyes opening and her gaze locking on his.

"Yes, I do."

"What if I can't?" she said, her voice barely audible above the roar of the jet boat engine.

Duff strained to hear her words. "Can't what?" he asked.

"Can't have children?"

He almost laughed. She was worried she couldn't have children. He was worried she wouldn't live to find out. "My mother always told me *don't borrow trouble.* We deal with whatever happens when we know more about it. Just hang in there. We'll be in Limón soon. We'll get you to the hospital and you'll be just fine."

"Magnus," she said, her fingers squeezing his hand. "Thank you."

"For what?" he asked.

"For saving my life three times now."

His heart squeezed hard in his chest. Until she made it to the hospital and the doctor declared she'd live, he wasn't sure he'd saved her life at all.

"Sweetheart?"

"Mmmm," she responded, her eyes closed.

"Care to try another date with this Delta Force soldier? I can't promise it'll be as exciting as the first two."

She smiled, her eyes still closed. "I'll take my chances."

"Is that a yes?"

She opened her eyes and smiled into his. "Yes."

"I'd kiss you, but I might injure you more with the boat moving like it is."

Her grin broadened briefly. "Save some for later. I need a nap."

She closed her eyes and didn't open them again until they transferred her to the ambulance waiting at the dock in Limón. Along with the ambulance was the entire team, armed to the gills, along with the Limón police.

"We would have called in the Costa Rican army," Lefty said. "But they don't have one."

It didn't matter. The cartel didn't make an appearance at the dock, en route to the hospital, or at the hospital.

The doctors took Ivy into surgery immediately.

While he sat in the surgical waiting room, Duff thought through all Ivy had said on the boat ride to Limón. She was worried that he'd be disappointed if she couldn't have children.

Did that mean she was thinking long-term about their relationship?

"Funny how Ivy was worried about having kids, isn't it?" Zip asked.

Duff frowned. "Why is that funny?"

"I mean, you two have only known each other a grand total of what...three days?"

"So?" Duff's frown deepened.

Zip held up his hands. "Just sayin' it hasn't been that long and she's already planning your family. How do you feel about that?"

"Honored, excited, blessed," he answered without hesitation. "How should I feel?"

Zip grinned. "I'll be damned."

"Why the hell should you be damned?" Duff demanded.

"It's true." His grin broadened. "The bigger they are, the harder they fall."

Duff was wound up tighter than a baby rattler

with a new button. "What the hell are you talking about?"

"You're in love with Ivy," Woof interjected.

"Right!" Zip said.

Woof's statement hit Duff square in the gut, knocking the wind out of him.

He was in love with Ivy.

Holy shit. When the hell had that happened?

He knew as soon as the thought came to him. He'd fallen for her the moment she'd landed in his arms in Gwen's bookstore.

The thought that he almost lost her the way he'd lost Katie, and that he could still lose her if something happened during surgery, broke him open.

"What's wrong, man?" Zip asked.

"First love will hit you like that," Woof said.

"She's not my first love," Duff said.

His teammates grew serious as they stared at him.

So Duff told them about Katie.

Finished telling his biggest secret, his head spinning, he almost didn't see the doctor walking through the waiting room door.

"She's out," Merlin said.

The team stood as one and converged on the doctor. He'd come out to report that she had come through just fine and that the bullet hadn't damaged any vital organs, including her reproductive system.

Duff smiled. That would make Ivy happy. He

didn't care if she never had children as long as she lived. They could always adopt.

"Can we see her?"

"Only one visitor, *por favor*," the doctor said.

Duff followed the doctor out of the waiting room. A nurse met him in the hallway and led him to Ivy's recovery room.

She was just coming out of the anesthesia when he approached her bed.

"Well?" she said, her voice gravelly, her eyes still droopy.

"You'll live," he said and took the hand without the IV stuck in it.

"I figured that when I woke."

"The bullet missed all your vital organs," Duff said.

"I can have children?" she asked, a smile blooming on her face.

Duff's heart burst open at her smile. "Yes, you can have as many as you like."

"I always wanted half a dozen," she said, closing her eyes. "Is that a problem?"

"No, sweetheart," he said. "I love you. And I'd love to have as many children as you want. I'll even change diapers."

"It's a good thing. If we're having a half a dozen, we have to get started. I'm not getting any younger."

He laughed. "Could we at least wait until your stitches heal?"

With her eyes still closed, she patted the bed beside her. "No time like the present, soldier."

Duff grinned. "You're not going to remember this conversation when the effects of the anesthesia wear off."

"Wanna bet?" she whispered and fell asleep.

He stayed with her until the nurse chased him out of the room that night.

He slept on the floor outside her room, still dressed in his tropical shirt and shorts with the tote bag carrying his Glock. He'd be damned if they'd come this far and someone slipped through his team guarding the hospital to get inside and hurt or kidnap her while she was recovering from a goddamn gunshot wound.

The next day, the doctor released her from the hospital. Senator Fremont had arranged for a medical transport plane to meet the ambulance at the airport and take her back to the States.

Duff insisted on flying back with her. The senator agreed wholeheartedly.

The rest of the team flew home in the back of the C130 that had delivered them to Limón, giving Duff hell over his first-class flight home.

The medical staff on board the private jet kept Ivy doped up with pain meds until she arrived back in Killeen, where she was transported to a local hospital with a surgical staff on-call to check her over.

They kept her overnight, weaning her off the

heavy doses of pain meds so that by the morning, she was fairly clear-headed and ready to go home.

Her mother arrived in time to speak with the doctor outside Ivy's room. When they were done, she turned to Duff. "Magnus. Thank you and your team for all you did to bring my daughter home."

He nodded. "She's a fighter, ma'am."

The senator nodded. The circles beneath her eyes told of the strain she'd been under. "Like her father."

"And her mother," he said.

She held out her hand. "I hope to see more of you in the future."

"You can count on it, ma'am. If your daughter agrees."

"She better," she said with a smile. "She could do a lot worse. None of the men she dated at the law firm were suitable. None of them had the fortitude and honor you and your team have in your pinky fingers. I'm glad she met you and I hope things work out between you."

"I'll work on it, ma'am."

"Make her work for it, too. You can't make it too easy or she'll know something's up." She winked and pulled on his hand, bringing him in for a hug. "Now, I'm going to see my daughter, and then I need to get her home to recover."

"Your place or hers?" he asked.

"She insisted on hers."

"Have you taken care of your situation? Will she remain in danger?"

The senator's eyes narrowed. "Not for much longer. There are government forces at work as we speak to take care of the problem now that we know where it is."

"Good." He nodded his head toward Ivy's door. "If it's all the same to you, I'd like to stay with Ivy until we know for certain the problem won't recur."

"Since I have to get back to Washington tomorrow, I'd like for you to stay as well," her mother said.

Duff's lip's twitched. "Now, all we have to do is get Ivy to agree."

"I heard that," Ivy called out through the open door of her room. "And yes, I agree."

Duff went to Ivy's bedside, taking her hand in his. "Hey," she said.

"Hey."

"I seem to keep waking up in strange places. Please, tell me I'm not in Costa Rica anymore."

He laughed. "You're in Killeen and you have a visitor." He stepped away, allowing her mother to approach the bed.

"Hi, baby girl," the senator said, taking her daughter's hand. "You go to a lot of lengths to get your mother to pay a personal visit to you, don't you?"

"Hi, Mom. You haven't called me baby girl since before Dad died."

She nodded. "I hadn't almost lost my baby girl

until now. It makes a senator rethink her priorities. Think I need to retire and spend more time with my family."

Ivy's brow furrowed. "Who's this woman and what have you done with my mother?"

"I deserved that."

Ivy shook her head. "No, Mother, you are doing what you do best. You're fighting for our country in Congress. I'll be here when you can make it home."

"But I want to be around to get to know my grandchildren."

"You can reevaluate your duties to the country when that time comes," Ivy said, her gaze going to Duff. She mouthed the words, *half a dozen,* and winked. "I remembered."

Duff laughed. "Yes, you did."

Her mother looked from her to Duff and back. "Am I missing the joke?"

"You won't for long if Ivy gets her way. And you'll be retiring before you know it."

Ivy's mother continued to frown, then shook her head and replaced the frown with a smile. "I'll leave you two alone while I arrange for the car to pick you up at the exit."

Ivy held onto her mother's hand a little longer. "I love you, Mom, and I'm proud of what you do."

Her mother nodded. "I love you, too. And if running a gift shop is what you want to do, I'm all for it. Life's too short to be in a job you hate."

When Ivy's mother left the room, Duff bent and kissed her lips. "I have more where that came from," he said.

"Good, because we have a lot of catching up to do. If I'm going to have half a dozen kids before I turn forty, we have to get cracking."

He chuckled. "It's not a race," he reminded her. "You're still recovering from a gunshot wound."

"I'm thirty. Forty is just around the corner." She frowned. "Wait. Am I scaring you?"

He shook his head. "Not at all. What scared me was seeing you lying on the seat of that boat, bleeding, knowing I hadn't stopped that bullet from hitting you."

"Oh, sweetie, you did the best you could. I didn't jump fast enough. And it was a lucky shot. If he'd been aiming, he would have missed." She winked. "Get me home, now, will ya? I think we can start work on that litter of babies we want tonight."

Duff kissed her long and hard, careful not to bump the cut on her temple or the stitches in her back.

If making babies was what Ivy wanted, he'd be happy to oblige. "I'm game on one condition," he said.

"And that is?" she asked.

"You marry me before the first one is born."

Ivy's eyes filled with tears. "Are you asking me to marry you?"

He tilted his head, a frown pulling at his brow.

"The words marry and me were strung together in the same sentence. I'd say that was what I was doing. But wait. Let me do this right." He winked and sank to one knee. "Ivy Fremont, will you make an honest man out of me and become my wife?"

Her brow puckered and more tears slipped from the corners of her eyes. "Are you sure that's what you want? You're not just asking because you feel sorry for me since you let me get shot?"

He sucked in a breath and let it out. "I'm on one knee. I just asked you to marry me, and I don't do anything I don't absolutely believe in. So, what's it to be?"

"Yes!" her mother said from the doorway. "She says yes."

Duff and Ivy looked toward the senator.

Her mother had the grace to blush. "I'm sorry. Of course, my daughter needs to be the one to agree. You agree, don't you, dear?"

Ivy turned to Duff. "You know when you marry a girl you inherit her mother, don't you?"

He nodded.

"Do you want to retract your offer?" Ivy asked.

"Ivy Nicole Fremont," her mother exclaimed. "Don't give the boy an out. He's asking, for the love of God. Say yes."

"Waiting," Duff prompted.

"You haven't changed your mind?" Ivy asked.

"No."

Her face split in a grin. "Yes!"

Duff rose from his knee and carefully gathered Ivy in his arms. "I love you, Ivy."

"I love you, too, Magnus McCormick."

He had the woman he loved, she'd agreed to marry him and have six children. Life didn't get any better than this.

The senator crossed the room and wrapped her arms around the two of them. "You two make me believe in love again." She wiped a tear from her eye and straightened. "Just so you both know. I got word, the DEA in coordination with the Limón police force captured the kingpin and a dozen members of the cartel orchestrating the transfer of drugs coming from Columbia to Costa Rica into the United States. The kingpin was the man who put the hits out on me and Ivy for stopping the sale of arms to him. He's being extradited to the States as we speak."

That's good news," Duff said.

She smoothed her hands over her skirt suit and squared her shoulders. "So, Ivy, you're safe." She clapped her hands like a high school football coach. "Now hurry up and get well. We have a wedding to plan and grandchildren to produce."

Beau "Jangles" Talbot sat on the edge of his bed, looked down at the long, wavy brown hair splashed across the pillowcase, and the area around his heart constricted.

"Babe?" he called and watched as she stirred but did not wake.

I need to end this.

He knew it, but he wasn't going to.

"Hope, baby, wake up," he tried again, and swept the heavy fall of hair off her bare shoulder.

The pads of his fingers skimmed over her warm, smooth skin. Hope opened her pretty brown eyes and Jangles fought the urge to crawl back into bed.

"Call out?" she mumbled.

"Yeah."

"Damn."

Damn was right. Since Jangles and his team

had transferred to Texas, they'd gone out frequently. Such was the life of a Special Operations Group. Terrorists didn't have a set schedule of operation. Extremist groups didn't limit their bombings to the hours between nine and five. And kidnappers and guerrilla forces didn't give the first fuck he was being pulled from his bed in the middle of the night. Further, they didn't care Jangles was leaving a sexy, hot, willing woman in that bed.

"You got Buster?" Jangles asked.

"You know I do. Go save the world."

No whiny complaints he was rolling out of bed. No bitching about where he was going or when he was coming back. No questions—period.

Just easy acceptance.

That was why he needed to end this.

Whatever *this* was, Jangles had to put a stop to it. He should've done it months ago. Hell, he never should've started it with Hope in the first place.

"I'll text you when we get back."

Hope's hand came up, her fingers stroked the side of his face, and her eyes gentled.

"Be safe, Beau."

That was why he hadn't ended it. Jangles was addicted to her gentle eyes and soft pleas for his safe return.

"Always am, babe. Go back to sleep."

Jangles leaned forward, kissed her shoulder, then

her forehead, and lingered just long enough to breathe her in.

Then he grabbed his bag and walked out the door, leaving Hope naked in his bed.

He did that, secure in the knowledge she'd be waiting for him when he got home. So he wasn't going to end it—proving he was a selfish prick, but not a stupid man. He knew Hope Mitchell was the best thing that had happened to him since he'd joined the Army.

*

BE sure to pick up the fifth and final book in the Delta Team Three series, Hope's Delta by Riley Edwards.

And if you haven't read the rest of the books in the series, I've included the links for all five stories.

Nori's Delta by Lori Ryan
Destiny's Delta by Becca Jameson
Gwen's Delta by Lynne St. James
Ivy's Delta by Elle James
Hope's Delta by Riley Edwards

Hellfire Series

Hellfire, Texas (#1)

Justice Burning (#2)

Smoldering Desire (#3)

Hellfire in High Heels (#4)

Playing With Fire (#5)

Up in Flames (#6)

Total Meltdown (#7)

Declan's Defenders

Marine Force Recon (#1)

Show of Force (#2)

Full Force (#3)

Driving Force (#4)

Tactical Force (#5)

Disruptive Force (#6)

Mission: Six

One Intrepid SEAL

Two Dauntless Hearts

Three Courageous Words

Four Relentless Days

Five Ways to Surrender

Six Minutes to Midnight

Hot Combat (#1)

Hot Target (#2)

Hot Zone (#3)

Hot Velocity (#4)

Cajun Magic Mystery Series

Voodoo on the Bayou (#1)

Voodoo for Two (#2)

Deja Voodoo (#3)

Cajun Magic Mysteries Books 1-3

SEAL Of My Own

Navy SEAL Survival

Navy SEAL Captive

Navy SEAL To Die For

Navy SEAL Six Pack

Devil's Shroud Series

Deadly Reckoning (#1)

Deadly Engagement (#2)

Deadly Liaisons (#3)

Deadly Allure (#4)

Deadly Obsession (#5)

Deadly Fall (#6)

Covert Cowboys Inc Series

Triggered (#1)

Taking Aim (#2)

Bodyguard Under Fire (#3)

Cowboy Resurrected (#4)

Navy SEAL Justice (#5)

Navy SEAL Newlywed (#6)

High Country Hideout (#7)

Clandestine Christmas (#8)

Thunder Horse Series

Hostage to Thunder Horse (#1)

Thunder Horse Heritage (#2)

Thunder Horse Redemption (#3)

Christmas at Thunder Horse Ranch (#4)

Demon Series

Hot Demon Nights (#1)

Demon's Embrace (#2)

Tempting the Demon (#3)

Lords of the Underworld

Witch's Initiation (#1)

Witch's Seduction (#2)

The Witch's Desire (#3)

Possessing the Witch (#4)

Stealth Operations Specialists (SOS)

Nick of Time

Alaskan Fantasy

Blown Away

Boys Behaving Badly Anthology

Rogues (#1)

Blue Collar (#2)

Pirates (#3)

Stranded (#4)

First Responder (#5)

Warrior's Conquest

Enslaved by the Viking Short Story

Conquests

Smokin' Hot Firemen

Protecting the Colton Bride

Protecting the Colton Bride & Colton's Cowboy Code

Heir to Murder

Secret Service Rescue

High Octane Heroes

Haunted

Engaged with the Boss

Cowboy Brigade

Time Raiders: The Whisper

ABOUT THE AUTHOR

ELLE JAMES also writing as MYLA JACKSON is a *New York Times* and *USA Today* Bestselling author of books including cowboys, intrigues and paranormal adventures that keep her readers on the edges of their seats. When she's not at her computer, she's traveling, snow skiing, boating, or riding her ATV, dreaming up new stories. Learn more about Elle James at www.ellejames.com

Website | Facebook | Twitter | GoodReads |
Newsletter | BookBub | Amazon

Or visit her alter ego Myla Jackson at
mylajackson.com
Website | Facebook | Twitter | Newsletter

Follow Me!
www.ellejames.com
ellejames@ellejames.com

There are many more books in this fan fiction world than listed here, for an up-to-date list go to www.AcesPress.com

Special Forces: Operation Alpha World

Christie Adams: Charity's Heart

Denise Agnew: Dangerous to Hold

Shauna Allen: Awakening Aubrey

Brynne Asher: Blackburn

Linzi Baxter: Unlocking Dreams

Jennifer Becker: Hiding Catherine

Alice Bello: Shadowing Milly

Heather Blair: Rescue Me

Anna Blakely: Rescuing Gracelynn

Julia Bright: Saving Lorelei

Cara Carnes: Protecting Mari

Kendra Mei Chailyn: Beast

Melissa Kay Clarke: Rescuing Annabeth

Samantha A. Cole: Handling Haven

Sue Coletta: Hacked

Melissa Combs: Gallant

Anne Conley: Redemption for Misty

KaLyn Cooper: Rescuing Melina

Liz Crowe: Marking Mariah

Sarah Curtis: Securing the Odds

Jordan Dane: Redemption for Avery

Tarina Deaton: Found in the Lost

Aspen Drake, Intense

KL Donn: Unraveling Love

Riley Edwards: Protecting Olivia

PJ Fiala: Defending Sophie

Nicole Flockton: Protecting Maria

Michele Gwynn: Rescuing Emma

Casey Hagen: Shielding Nebraska

Desiree Holt: Protecting Maddie

Kathy Ivan: Saving Sarah

Kris Jacen, Be With Me

Jesse Jacobson: Protecting Honor

Silver James: Rescue Moon

Becca Jameson: Saving Sofia

Kate Kinsley: Protecting Ava

Heather Long: Securing Arizona

Gennita Low: No Protection

Kirsten Lynn: Joining Forces for Jesse

Margaret Madigan: Bang for the Buck

Kimberly McGath: The Predecessor

Rachel McNeely: The SEAL's Surprise Baby

KD Michaels: Saving Laura

Lynn Michaels, Rescuing Kyle

Wren Michaels: The Fox & The Hound

Kat Mizera: Protecting Bobbi

Keira Montclair, Wolf and the Wild Scots

Mary B Moore: Force Protection

LeTeisha Newton: Protecting Butterfly

Angela Nicole: Protecting the Donna

MJ Nightingale: Protecting Beauty

Sarah O'Rourke: Saving Liberty

Victoria Paige: Reclaiming Izabel

Anne L. Parks: Mason
Debra Parmley: Protecting Pippa
Lainey Reese: Protecting New York
TL Reeve and Michele Ryan: Extracting Mateo
Elena M. Reyes: Keeping Ava
Angela Rush: Charlotte
Rose Smith: Saving Satin
Jenika Snow: Protecting Lily
Lynne St. James: SEAL's Spitfire
Dee Stewart: Conner
Harley Stone: Rescuing Mercy
Jen Talty: Burning Desire
Reina Torres, Rescuing Hi'ilani
Savvi V: Loving Lex
Megan Vernon: Protecting Us
Rachel Young: Because of Marissa

Delta Team Three Series
Lori Ryan: Nori's Delta
Becca Jameson: Destiny's Delta
Lynne St James, Gwen's Delta
Elle James: Ivy's Delta
Riley Edwards: Hope's Delta

Police and Fire: Operation Alpha World
Freya Barker: Burning for Autumn
BP Beth: Scott
Julia Bright, Justice for Amber
Anna Brooks, Guarding Georgia

KaLyn Cooper: Justice for Gwen
Aspen Drake: Sheltering Emma
Deanndra Hall: Shelter for Sharla
Barb Han: Kace
EM Hayes: Gambling for Ashleigh
CM Steele: Guarding Hope
Reina Torres: Justice for Sloane
Aubree Valentine, Justice for Danielle
Maddie Wade: Finding English
Stacey Wilk: Stage Fright
Laine Vess: Justice for Lauren

Tarpley VFD Series
Silver James, Fighting for Elena
Deanndra Hall, Fighting for Carly
Haven Rose, Fighting for Calliope
MJ Nightingale, Fighting for Jemma
TL Reeve, Fighting for Brittney
Nicole Flockton, Fighting for Nadia

As you know, this book included at least one character from Susan Stoker's books. To check out more, see below.

SEAL of Protection: Legacy Series
Securing Caite
Securing Brenae (novella)
Securing Sidney
Securing Piper
Securing Zoey
Securing Avery
Securing Kalee (Sept 2020)
Securing Jane (Feb 2021)

SEAL Team Hawaii Series
Finding Elodie (Apr 2021)
Finding Lexie (Aug 2021)
Finding Kenna (Oct 2021)
Finding Monica (TBA)
Finding Carly (TBA)
Finding Ashlyn (TBA)

Delta Team Two Series
Shielding Gillian
Shielding Kinley (Aug 2020)
Shielding Aspen (Oct 2020)
Shielding Riley (Jan 2021)

Shielding Devyn (May 2021)
Shielding Ember (Sep 2021)
Shielding Sierra (TBA)

Delta Force Heroes Series

Rescuing Rayne (FREE!)
Rescuing Aimee (novella)
Rescuing Emily
Rescuing Harley
Marrying Emily (novella)
Rescuing Kassie
Rescuing Bryn
Rescuing Casey
Rescuing Sadie (novella)
Rescuing Wendy
Rescuing Mary
Rescuing Macie (Novella)

Badge of Honor: Texas Heroes Series

Justice for Mackenzie (FREE!)
Justice for Mickie
Justice for Corrie
Justice for Laine (novella)
Shelter for Elizabeth
Justice for Boone
Shelter for Adeline
Shelter for Sophie
Justice for Erin
Justice for Milena

Shelter for Blythe
Justice for Hope
Shelter for Quinn
Shelter for Koren
Shelter for Penelope

SEAL of Protection Series

Protecting Caroline (FREE!)
Protecting Alabama
Protecting Fiona
Marrying Caroline (novella)
Protecting Summer
Protecting Cheyenne
Protecting Jessyka
Protecting Julie (novella)
Protecting Melody
Protecting the Future
Protecting Kiera (novella)
Protecting Alabama's Kids (novella)
Protecting Dakota

New York Times, USA Today and *Wall Street Journal*
Bestselling Author Susan Stoker has a heart as big as
the state of Tennessee where she lives, but this all
American girl has also spent the last fourteen years
living in Missouri, California, Colorado, Indiana, and
Texas. She's married to a retired Army man who now
gets to follow *her* around the country.

BOOKS BY SUSAN STOKER

www.stokeraces.com
www.AcesPress.com
susan@stokeraces.com